THE
n-BODY
PROBLEM

TONY BURGESS

ChiZine Publications

For Jake and Emily

FIRST EDITION

The n-Body Problem © 2013 by Tony Burgess
Cover artwork © 2013 by Erik Mohr
Interior design © 2013 by Samantha Beiko
Interior illustrations © 2013 by Jason Brown

Distributed in Canada by
HarperCollins Canada Ltd.
1995 Markham Road
Scarborough, ON M1B 5M8
Toll Free: 1-800-387-0117
e-mail: hcorder@harpercollins.com

Distributed in the U.S. by
Diamond Book Distributors
1966 Greenspring Drive
Timonium, MD 21093
Phone: 1-410-560-7100 x826
e-mail: books@diamondbookdistributors.com

Library and Archives Canada Cataloguing in Publication Data

Burgess, Tony, 1959-, author
   The n-body problem / Tony Burgess.

Issued in print and electronic formats.
ISBN 978-1-77148-163-2 (pbk.).-- ISBN 978-1-77148-164-9 (pdf)

   I. Title.

PS8553.U63614N36 2013   C813'.54   C2013-905156-2

                              C2013-905157-0

CHIZINE PUBLICATIONS
Toronto, Canada
www.chizinepub.com
info@chizinepub.com

Edited and copyedited by Brett Savory
Proofread by Kelsi Morris

Canada Council   Conseil des Arts
for the Arts   du Canada

We acknowledge the support of the Canada Council for the Arts which last year
invested $20.1 million in writing and publishing throughout Canada.

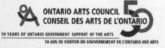

ONTARIO ARTS COUNCIL
CONSEIL DES ARTS DE L'ONTARIO
50 YEARS OF ONTARIO GOVERNMENT SUPPORT OF THE ARTS
50 ANS DE SOUTIEN DU GOUVERNEMENT DE L'ONTARIO AUX ARTS

Published with the generous assistance of the Ontario Arts Council.

THE
n-BODY
PROBLEM

jq$_k$under|, q$_j$umlaut=1| $\underline{m}_j\Sigma$,, |q$_j$umlautq$_k$underG, -under| q$_k$underq$_j$umlautq$_j\Sigma$)

A completed Craft Project Assignment for the Holiday Arts Mail Order School

$$G\Sigma| \ \Sigma_- \ )==q_k \text{under}| \ )m_j =_- \ \underline{m}_k$$
$$m_j , \quad = m_j | = \Sigma| \quad m_j |G \quad (j$$
$$,=1(j, \quad \underline{m}_k \ ()$$

i am not my own food.

Insomnia, for instance, is a death sentence. Used to be the occasional genetic syndrome, Fatal Familial Insomnia, things like that. One in a million. Not now. Now you stop sleeping because you thought a bit too long. It frightened you. And you felt it, maybe while you were doing something else, you slipped . . . you thought about it . . . pictures on the wall . . . suspended with what? Hooks? Hangers? Staples? Nails? What? You push them into the wall with your own strength . . . like a pea into gravy. Swallow by the wall. A bird entered a cloud. And none of it. Not one stick of light or dark had a thing to do with sleep. That's how you do it. You don't change the picture. You destroy picturing.

It is probably because of the sky that we now walk looking down. We focus our eyes on the hard imperfect dirt, the anamorphic islands in hardwood slats, the infant memory picked into marks on linoleum. In fact, so obsessed have we become in reading the flat earth that we now bump into each other more often, and we are warned about this danger, we are told to look up, not high not above us, but in front, so we can see obstacles, see the things we want, the place we are going; so we may read the world as nature had intended us to, as something before us. For many people the problem then becomes one of scale. The cracks become canyons, the piece of glass a crystal mountain. There is great wrong in this, and we know it—a grain of sand wasn't given to us to carry on our backs like beasts, we were not put here to drag cherries by the stem. But now, it is the dream we dream. It is our wish to be as far away from the sky as possible, to soak our perspective in the fizz under rotting leaves. And so we stare downward as we walk, judging the things around us like bats do, and we fail, slapping into poles and posts and each other. It's a price we grimly accept, to look upward as little as we can. To be concentrating on a place we are not, but could be, were we only so much smaller, so much farther from the sky.

The sky is there, though, perhaps even more there than ever, since it is the pressure that has stuck our eyes with push pins into the lawn. The sky is the power over us, it is what makes us want to live so far away from what we are. People have stabbed themselves, forks in the eyes, skewers through the ears, some have shoved ropes down their throats and poured hot glue across their eyelids. I try to do my best, looking outward, I'm still approved for SSRIs and mild anti-psychotics, so I'm still finding solutions day to day, moment by moment. I've kept the docs in the dark about the serotonin syndrome I can feel growing. It's another obsessive scale to avoid. Nerve endings, neurotransmitters deformed by clouds of serotonin. It's hard to resist sometimes, being a fighter pilot on a synthetic molecule with shape dive-bombing receptors, living life like this, in a skyless, groundless wobble of shapes warring with each other, desperate to recognize a recess somewhere, anywhere that resembles my ship, so I can plug myself in once and for all and be made warm and light and essential.

You can desire life here, imagine it. The challenges are great but you have leather boots on and a cap with swinging straps and you don't need to know if the world thinks you're a hero or not. You are. You are because you don't care if you live or die. And that is better than walking down a street, clenching and unclenching your fists in the hope that you can bring wellness back into them. That is hopeless. If you feel cancer and childishness is where you are walking to, then all is lost. Nothing is possible. It is always and forever better to have never been born.

prisoners of love.

It's been a year and a half since Orbit.

On Wednesday next, the number will reach and pass one billion. Somewhere above us—you can find out where online—a cold graphite chamber pot the size of an aircraft carrier is turning on the soft directing puffs of tiny jets. Getting into position to release its cargo along a mathematically perfect slipstream. A hundred and twenty thousand or so bodies will drift out like soda from an airborne can and find themselves lying in a row beside others. Among them is the billionth. One billion bodies crisscrossing the stratosphere in a perfect careful lattice, its depth controlled, its rigid vectors held apart by mere feet. One billion is the big number.

I set up this thing tonight, at the Jubilee Church.

Father and son potluck. No ladies. Split the families up. For what? I don't get it and I don't care. I've seen religious types that are worse. Far worse. All I need now is a son.

I found a bed and breakfast joint. Fancy frilly old house run by a couple real frail birds. Paula and Petra or something like that. One of them paints a lot of birds. There's framed watercolours all over the house. Robins mostly. Stuff my son could do if I had one. I can hear the girls moving around in the kitchen. They're quiet. Bird-like. Things are placed silently in drawers. Petra? Is that her name? The mirror in my room is the size of a wall. It's got this wood frame and feet and it leans. I look derailed today. Hair all jackknifed up and a bright red pattern on my cheek. What is that? Rosacea, I'd say. As if that's even something I'd worry about. No. I lean in. That's the impression of a doily. I glance back at the fussy pillow sleeves. The light in this room is like horse piss. Everything is splashing up off the floor, down the walls. Lice on the pillows. No. SARS. Influenza. Maybe. Not today, but chances are at one time. I hate this light. Big enough to cast a buffalo shadow off a cluster fly. Not full spectrum of course, that sort of light is rare. This is stick-on light. Couple years back everything got a feel-better facelift. As if we could trap sunlight in cheerful plastics. Yellow everywhere. And commercials promising a "mood lift" like we could be driving around in Prozac cars. In fact, the colours have a pharmaceutical look, pale orange bars, powder blue bevels. Lots of cream with small red letters. I think the colours in this room predate that, though. This is old-folk cheer. It acts like happy is not going to fly out the window. But it did, didn't it? Turns out happy was a thing just like everything else and it can leave an entire planet. Thinning and dispersing. All the earth happy, now just cold balls of paper caught in solar winds and comet tails.

"Mr. Cauldwell?"

That's either Petra or Paula. Am I even remembering those names? I flip open the pill box. Takes me three mouthfuls to get all my meds down. I could tell you what they are, what they are for, but that could all change by later today. You have to keep mind/body/pharma pretty dynamic these days. I can hear the girls' voices. Little bird noises. This flophouse is a damn birdhouse.

"I'll be down in sec."

My belt is twisted at my back. I'm too lazy to fix it. It will pinch the skin all day. I've gained some weight. That's fine. Needing to lose weight is far better than needing to find it again. I'm bigger than the disease. At least for today.

I can smell toast. Going downstairs I straighten a pencil sketch of a hummingbird. The blurry wings are a cheap effect done with an eraser. Looks stupid. At the bottom of the stairs I get a shock. Paula and Petra are Asian. I had to have known that. My chest starts to tighten. It is dangerous to go off-road right this second. It's a lapse. Just thinking it was one thing and it turns out to be another. I push my back muscles into the leather kink there. I am larger than memory problems. Liver disease can do this. Infections. Autoimmune flare ups. Spinal compression. Are their names even Petra and Paula? I can't give a fuck.

The ladies step back from me and pause. I sit observed. Toast, no butter, and hardboiled eggs.

"Are you working here today or out?"

It's a nervy question and I don't think I'll say. The other Paula and Petra steps forward to correct.

"We are going out today, so if you need lunch we'll put it in the fridge."

There's a piece of eggshell stabbing below my gum line. Shell and tooth. There are infections of the gums that are fatal. The shell of a bird's egg is separating the gum from tooth. I smell copper. There's enough blood in my mouth that I can smell it. I have to excuse myself. I have to find a boy to be my son tonight.

parts.

I cut through some backyards. Not many sidewalks in these small towns. Birdhouses for people line the streets. White doilies and an orange film on windows from days when poison was legal.

The fountain's dry. I do that. I look for neglected things. Not uncommon to see a flat tire on a new car. And the car just sits there. Dipped like a bad smile. I don't give a shit about it. The ground is rising and the sky is falling. It's okay to leave a few things lying around.

The grass is brown. I step onto the main street. Ontario towns look like a plate Lillian Gish keeps on the shelf. When the sun cuts through the drapes, it's the drapes that light us. She's probably watching right now. The boy I need to find. The son I should have. I have to borrow a child from the real world tonight. I'll put him back. Don't worry.

A young woman passes me. I cover my mouth instead of smile. She can't tell I didn't. There's tall buckets of pine ends. Carpenter. I stop to see. There's a lot of small cupboards. Unstained. More Gish. A metal fisherman with pinched seams. The cotton line to a silver trout. I do like looking. It keeps picturing at bay. The light must be constantly moving on this little guy. It is all suddenly happening in ways it can't happen. I turn to the barrel of pine ends. The smell cauterizes. No memory. No taste. No life. Just perfect tan caps on all the punched-out receptors. It's heaven to inhale this. Pine is clean. Pine is made of clean.

I don't know if that's anything. It's just a theory I have. Your brain can't be making shit up if you're carefully observing the things around you. This is a very aggressive hypochondria. Nobody escapes it in the end. You picture a tumour pressing up in your chest wall and soon, hours sometimes, your shoulder starts to prickle . . . the ulnar nerve lights up all the way down and spatulates your fingers. Then pica spots show up in the apex of a lung. Then you cough blood. Can't see a doctor. Doctor knocks symptoms off you like a dog shaking off wet.

Anyhow, trick is, I need a boy. Not hard to do, really. You just gotta have the nerve. And find the right mom.

I move across the street. Light mist in the air. Spring shower. I don't look up. More of these losers window shopping. Antique stores. Pet store. Pizza. These are peep shows for the dead. Take a look, folks. We used to have dazzling teeth. I always check the parked cars. Moms and boys sitting in cars. There. Bet they've been sitting there for days. I tap the window. The boy looks up. The mom just stares ahead. Perfect. I tap again and the window comes down. The smell of shit. That's common. Some folks, late in the game, start shitting themselves for protection. Doesn't make any sense to us, of course. She doesn't need a son. She needs a cocoon of feces.

Turns out I don't even have to ask. The kid jumps out of the car and his mother doesn't. That's the best way. I step back and walk down an alley. The kid follows. He's twelve or so. Means he can manoeuvre out of a jam but still can't overpower me. He smells like his mom, but I think he's generally clean. I turn a corner to the back of the pizza joint. There's a hose.

"Strip."

I unravel the first couple metres of hose. The boy's face is dull. He removes his shirt. This is gonna be a bit wild at first. I twist the handle. He stands straight and naked. I move him over to a grate and hit him with the water, making sure I got a firm hand on his wrist. He pops pretty good, like a hare. He lets out a screech so I hold the cold water on his face. He goes still. Bring the hose across the front of him, dislodging grey and black mould. Quick spin and rout his backside. Good enough. I squeeze the hose off. He's awake now. I cuff him to a bike rack.

"Don't make any noise."

Kid's perfect. No stupidity. I march up the alley. Need a second-hand clothes store. Stedmans. Something. Maybe get another kid just for his clothes. Jesus, the things you can manage to do if you want to. I glance over at the mom sitting in the car. That's ridiculous. Turn into a toy store. Maybe they got swim trunks. Towel. Boy scout uniform.

"G'day!"

Cheerful old bugger. Big thick glasses. Could be a mole. Hanging in there pretty fair though, I'd say.

"You got any kids clothes?"

I hear a little sigh. That's all. That's his disapproval.

banded.

Promise Keepers. They're every-where. Iron Men Male power. Better than the rapists, anyway. That was a dark couple of months. Everyone was a rapist. Just exploded. Not sure why. But it ended. I guess if you can picture what you want then eventually you'll picture what you don't want. Not only is rape off the menu, so is sex. All sex. Not one person has sex on the entire planet for about a full year. That's my take on it anyway. Sure there's probably a village somewhere in a valley where they fuck all day, but the species is terminal. Viagra has a cascading effect on symptoms, usually, skin cancers or inner ear things—Raynaud's. Sit there waiting for your dick to rise and watch the lesions split open on your thighs. Oh, yes. We are terminal. That's what happens when you fuck with light.

Men-only dinner at the Evangelical Hall. You

need a son to get in. And a meatloaf. I picked that up at a Dairy Queen. Technically it's burger meat pounded into a pan. Same as meat loaf. The boy seems content enough to walk with me. Crisp little boy scout uniform on him. Clean body. Not a bad day for a child. We congregate in the basement. More of a gym. This is where I'm looking for my guy. A rare person he is. He steals. He kills. Not many of them left. He organizes suicide cults. For some reason fathers and sons are easy marks. Teenagers a close second. Who knows why we're like this now? The studies aren't getting done any more. Nobody knows me here, but really they all do.

I slide my pan onto a counter with the other pans.

There are three long tables set up. Forks, spoons, knives. Ketchup. Men sitting, looking alive for the most part. You can see some infections. Bad ones. Ears running. There's one guy being led to the table by a boy. Eyes are fog-white. Glaucoma maybe. Bet he didn't have that when he woke up this morning. No cancer anyway. You can smell that shit. Kills within hours.

Not much eye contact here. Fit-looking elder lining the pans of meat on a table. Another, older man with a stoop dishes out gravy with a ladle. The boys look anxious to get away. Not mine. He never leaves my side. The man I'm looking for will have found his son like I did. He'll fit in the way I

am. He knows fathers and sons are vulnerable, and these days anyway, likely to hold the family money. He also likes churches because he fancies himself a minister. He is a mechanism of God. He'll point out the obvious: the living are the suffering, the sinners. We have been left behind and above us, bathed in light and weightless, are the free. He will instruct them how to die and then get their signatures on certain documents. Then they will die and he will move on to another town. Steal another boy. Drift down into another potluck dinner for men. Combine their despair and emptiness like elements of a homemade bomb.

The fit elder sits across from me. He pokes the grey mass on his plate.

"Lotsa meat. No potatoes."

The elder looks at my boy.

"We know he's not your son."

I put my hand on the boy's shoulder.

"Well, you see—"

"It's ok. He's better off. That's all we need to know. My name's Russel."

Russel lays his hand, palm up, on the table. I'm not to shake it. I look at it then quickly brush my fingers across his.

"I'm looking for somebody, Russel."

"I know. He was here. We knew what he was about. No time for that here."

"Good for you."

"We used to do mission work. Irrigation systems. Help develop farmland in places like Ghana, West Africa. Them folks need our help."

Russel bows his head. Drops the hand to his lap.

"Now. Well. Now. We're just trying to remind our own to eat."

"Did he stay or move on?"

"Who? Oh, him. I think he's still in town. Going after teenagers. It's evil what these guys do. I guess the best lack all conviction."

I can't eat the food. It'd be a concern but I think it's just bad. Anorexia's a swamp of problems. You gotta carry around IV bags and shit.

"What he look like?"

Russel smiles when the boy takes a mouthful of the stiff white beef.

"Oh. Nothing remarkable about him. He had a boy, like you. Let's see. Thin fella. Sides of his head shaved."

"You notice anything about his hands?"

"Yes. That's right. The last digit on his small finger was gone. Hadda big yellow callous at the tip."

Some cells feel like they might be cracking open beside my spine. Ice water under my shoulder blade. I have to make a quick choice. Is it a tumour? No. Too unexpected. What then? The sensation is so vivid it's as if it's happening before my eyes. An injection of ice. Something has broken open. MS?

"You okay?"

The ice turns to grass fire. A surface fire. I adjust my shoulder slightly and feel a sewing machine sweep down my back.

Shingles. That's fuckin' hilarious. It even possible I got this honestly? Varicella zoster virus—chicken pox, sleeping in nerve ending by my spine, suddenly wakes up and stakes blisters on my flesh. Or. Or. What? Shingles weren't even on the radar.

"You okay? You're sweating."

I nod, sure. To prove this I fork some food to my mouth. A large droplet swings from my nose and hits the food. I can't even chew. My mouth retreats around the food. My tongue furls to the back. My teeth jump apart. The lump feels electrified. Time to go.

The boy sticks close as we climb up the church basement steps. Dark now. I have to take care of things. I drop the food from my mouth and spit. The flame in my spine trips again and I flinch my way to Main Street.

Trying to remember which side of the street I got the boy from. Going to return him before things get too crazy. I peer in the car. The smell of shit sticks to the window. Can't tell if Mom's expired or just catatonic. Anyhow. Family reunion. I pull a twenty out and stuff it in the boy's pants. Open the door.

What hits us isn't an odour; it's a force. The woman's dead. Her lower half has dissolved. I shut the door, and watch a whirl of coloured air warp the sidewalk.

I don't look at the boy. Sometimes doing no wrong means doing no right. I open the rear door, hoping the seat is dry. I gesture to the boy. You're home, buddy. Thanks for hanging out.

He looks at me, then extends his hand. I shake it. He climbs into the back seat and I slam the door.

He knows I helped. A meal. Shower. New clothes. I do him one last favour.

His mother is moving. She won't hurt him, but she's not gonna stop moving either. She's dead. She'll eventually shimmy to the floor and agitate all the poison. I hold my breath and open the driver door. Grab her by the coat and pull. She hits the road like a bad pumpkin. Then I swing her to the sidewalk. As much of her as holds together. There must be roadside pickup but I don't know the day. Not perfectly legal what I'm doing.

I take three long strides before I breathe. The sugary rot punches my gut. Too much sick to fight off. At least the shingles are buried by this.

Heading back to make a plan. There may be time to catch the Youth Drop-in tonight. I'm about to cross the street but I stop. Back to the car.

Can't leave the fuckin' kid like that.

he has brought the house down.

The guy with the sides of his head shaved. Mushroom cap on his little finger. That guy. You see, this racket is about going into communities, taking a few key people aside and talking them into killing themselves. The more marks you got the bigger the pile of gold they're gonna leave behind. And it's surprisingly easy to do. There just aren't that many people left who actually wanna be here and if the Seller can lull you a bit with the idea of sunbathing weightlessly in space, with the world rolling below, then you happily go. Sometimes the Seller convinces you that he'll go too. He doesn't though. He stays back and drains your dough, then moves on.

I know the Seller with the sides of his head shaved. That's Glenn Dixon. He's a top Seller. He once got a whole town—8,500 people—to lie down and die. Glenn and I go way back.

The boy and I keep up Main. It's about six o'clock. The Christian Drop-in opens at seven o'clock. I figure we'll sit in the parkette and watch folks for an hour. The boy is steady, calm. We sit on a bench by a fountain. I open some pills and gag a bit to get them down. The boy stares ahead. He's a remora. I'm a shark.

Bright fence line across my vision. Top left half is pinball. Like a layer of hallucination pulled itself between me and the savage world. A slicing pain around the left ear. I can feel that things I'm going to think about this won't add up. I have to affirm this temporarily. There are banana-coloured skies. There are crying leaves. There is a road that goes through puberty. Hot red teeth. Hallucinated light drawing shadows. That's it. That's what I affirm. The things that are not here are having a measurable effect on the things that are. If I look down, then eggs will fall from nests, pollen will bounce like flour on the lawn. Stroke. I don't know much. Strokes do damage. I press in and try to hold on. The pain pushes down. I can't swallow. There is one line, jagged and falling like a graph, a charted downturn. It's black with a red ghost line. This is the dominant. It denies contiguity. The world above it is charged with pain and light. It is a stylus. Below the world is cold. Pain free. I am not in this half. I have to be. A couple. No faces. Long legs walk at an angle and turn. They can't walk to a point. Not this point. Boot is a shadow club. I see the fine blue dots. Artefacts of her long coat. I need a place to store. I need a notebook. There is a finite number. She is an age. She is an entire morning. That. That is where I am not. That is where I am be. Raise my head quickly. Do the thing that things don't expect. You make them what they are. The effect is disastrously close to being permanent. I can't imagine and I feel sick. I throw up at my feet. The pain scoops my forehead. I watch the long line of yellow spin to the ground. My lip to a crack in stone. This could be the out. Stones. Small and unlike one another. They have come from places, moved here on the bottom of impressionable boots. Grains. Wind born from the gutter. A purple plastic dulled by sun and winter. Part of a bubble-blowing ring. It is enough. It is enough. I count the rows of dimples in stone anyway. I note flaws. I mark variations—depth, colour. One dimple is a wound. White in the centre. A ring of inflammation. I close my eyes and pray for some approximation, something independent, something less accurate. Fuck me. How are regular people supposed to handle this? It's hopeless. We need to be able to guess, for fuck's sake.

I have sat quietly for half an hour. The boy too.

He was patient while I suffered. Now I am sitting upright. I have good breathing. The pain is all old. Echo. I am less worried about formulating. Less obsessed. I have two things in my vision that I'll have to accept. One is a red and purple egg just off centre. The other is a thick line across the bottom. If I look up, the line widens. It looks like a face. Talking. If I look down, it disappears. Not gonna kill me. It's good to have reminders. Like an oil light on the dash. I see you but I can drive. Big road ahead. The boy is calm. His boy scout uniform looks ridiculous. I get up and he follows.

Short round Indian man in Stedmans. Behind him a rainbow of long shoehorns. Two feet long. He smiles and wheezes. Did you know that there are things about emphysema that are pleasurable? It's true. Your lungs can feel soft. Your body's gratitude for small oxygen is thrilling. You can feel great. I ask about kids clothes. He waves to a rack of things by the ties.

The kid is thin. I grab a t-shirt. Pale blue. Wolf. Nah.

"Pick something."

The kid looks up. He warily brushes the clothes. Performing, at first, self-conscious, then he makes a choice. I admire this. See who sees you. Then get what you want. He picks a plain brown t-shirt and some jeans. No socks, no underwear. The runners he has on are fine. He strips in the middle of the store and tosses the boy scout shit onto a table of candles. I catch the clerk watching us in the security mirror. Whatever, man. You look like a fuckin' duck.

The Youth Drop-in has been merged with an AA meeting in the back of an auto body shop. Teenagers and coffee-sipping drunks mix outside. In the past this would be a scene of terrible rape and probably beating. Maybe even death. Now, its all little cheese fingers and cigarette smoke stuck to faces. I wish the kid would talk. He has not spoken once.

I get through the small group and enter the building. It's a lunchroom for the employees. Chairs in a circle. Some pastries on a glass plate. I have to look down for a second to see a woman with long grey hair and a guitar. I gasp. The face opens up along that line again. That's going to bother me in time.

"Hi there. I'm Bob."

Not my name. The woman looks up, her face behind long grey hair.

"Well, hi, Bob. I'm Ashley."

We both look at the boy for a moment, then look away.

"You're welcome here."

There are slogans on the walls. A picture of Jesus.

"Really. You are."

I can't look down. The talking face is distracting.

Like a TV. I want to hear what's being said on it.

"Good. Thank you."

Still can't look. Makes it harder. I sit. There. The egg settles above the line. Fuckin' stroke.

"Can I ask you a question, Ashley?"

Ashley bangs a thumb softly on a string.

"Shoot."

"You know pretty much everybody who comes out to this?"

Ashley frowns deeply and thinks.

"The regulars. Yeah. Why? You looking for someone?"

I lean forward, elbows to knees. Ashley smiles at the kid.

"I am, yes. He's a thin guy. Gotta funny haircut."

Ashley gives me a hard look.

"That's weird. Why would you be looking for him?"

"You've seen him? You know him?"

Ashley appears to think again. A performance. Neurotic. She pretends to feel things. Acts like she knows.

"Nope. And I know everybody who comes to these meetings. Nobody new. Nobody different."

That's not what you said at first. Not precisely.

There's hollering outside. Ashley looks at me. She's still pretending to think about the guy I'm looking for. She thinks, then shakes her head no.

I don't like the hollering outside. Neither does the kid. He's turned in his chair. It's 6:45 p.m. The door opens. A teenage girl. She is dramatic. Old Fashioned.

"Chris is on the ground."

I stand outside the circle around Chris. He is having a seizure. It's raining. Warm rain. The kids are hugging each other and weeping. The drama teen is down beside Chris.

"No, Chris. No! You can't die! You can't! I'll never find you!"

Chris stops seizing. His hair is soaked. His face the colour of shrimp. He's sick alright. He's burning. I can see blood surfacing on his finger tips. He coughs up bright blood. One of his eyes slips below the socket. Thick fluids fill the space. This is viral. Virus is rare. A perfect storm. The receptors have to take territory in the stem cells. Your body has to make the virus. Give it life. Frankenstein. He coughs again and a mist of blood covers his forehead.

Since I'm not certain if these Frankensteins are physically present and therefore contagious, I push the boy back. I don't need to be here.

The boy and I slip away. The girl falls on Chris, wailing. We hear a muffled *plumph* noise then a scream. Some part of his body has just released contents on her.

at the back, the front.

Twenty years ago. That's when people stopped dying properly. They were dead inasmuch as they stopped being people. But they were alive because they never ceased to move. They didn't walk. They didn't do things. They just moved. A strange gentle agitation. Like Parkinson's disease that kept on post-mortem.

At first, we were terrified of them. We thought they would kill us. I don't know why. We thought that the only reason the dead aren't dead is because they wanted to kill us. So, we waged war on them. Shooting them and setting them on fire. We ran from them. We quarantined people in stadiums. We believed that terrible violent things were happening. It was often repeated on the news—the dead were eating us. In time their numbers grew. The dead were forming enormous masses. Twitching masses. All across the world. In time, economies began to collapse. Wars ended quietly. Leaders slipped away. We didn't totally cave in. Some took hold of the structures, the culture, the daily life and they looked past, believing this was a solvable problem. They noticed, and soon we all did, that the dead were not hurting us. They were harmless.

It took a long time for this fact to spread into the population. Some never bought it and committed horrible acts of hate on the dead. Some destroyed the dead for sport. Some kept parts in collections. Some wore moving fingers on chains. Still do. There's a complicated, deviant culture pretty much everywhere these days.

When some calm returned, when a majority was finally convinced that the dead meant no harm—in fact, meant nothing—then solutions became possible. This was a waste disposal problem. The dead numbered in the many hundreds of millions. And they made up mountains of bodies. Like water droplets running into each other to create flowing water. They didn't mean to hurt us, but they threatened life in other ways. They became immovable. We didn't know it at first but their biggest threat was invisible: we were now, all of us, thinking about them and thinking about them all the time.

Governments, or at least what was left of them, turned to the private sector for tenders. Dispose of these things in an efficient and reasonable way. Keep costs down. Make it sustainable. Many proposals became popular. At one time, enormous cremating ovens were erected in Africa. They had incredible capacity. They recorded over a hundred thousand cremations a day. It was impressive. Iron ovens the size of cruise liners. Clean white smoke woven in the clouds. Still, weightless ash flowing on the wind into desert lands.

It was the pictures that killed it though. Bulldozed bodies piled in the ovens. The filthy heat and fire. It was, to many, a ghost. The holocaust. The iron cross and the metal letters. There were others who saw the bodies burn and believed we were constructing hell. We were Satan's architects and builders. Others, sentimental ones, just couldn't bear the thought of an uncle or sister twitching in the dark centres of these body balls, then being burned.

The African ovens were abandoned. There was a flood of proposals. Weight them down at the bottom of the Marianas Trench. This one failed in trials. The bodies simply found ways to surface. A clip of a trawler cutting through a sea of moving flesh and faces as far as the eye could see was too much. Landfill projects were tried, but with similar results. Thousands of moving beings beneath a landscape will find a way to break the surface. They poured down from hills and parks. Science tried to still them. To make them stop. But even this was too offensive once we saw their work. Vivisection and freezing and hammering and encasing and draining and filling with hard glues. Nothing stopped our nightmares. We were starting to feel this new creature was lying within us.

The answer that we finally accepted went like this. Waste Management Corp. (WasteCorp) constructed space shuttles with immense crates on their backs. These ships headed into our upper atmosphere and released the millions, setting them into orbit around the earth. WasteCorp, having learned a few things, knew it had to calm us, had to provide new rituals, had to give us the right pictures. Sunbaked loved ones. Star-dappled children. Not gathering in mounds like mad insects, but rather distributed evenly in infinite space. Great care was taken with both word and image. In fact, it was pitched as a vast improvement over being eaten by worms in the cold, indifferent earth. This was a room with a view. This was not death, but like what it was, a final place to slow down and be surrounded by wonder.

And so we sent them. By the millions. The only

images we saw were beautiful. People leaving the ship easily, then drifting like a soft astral landscape. There was no question: it was the perfect place to rest. WasteCorp said that the dead were gently refusing the grave, and waiting for us to move them to the sky. If you could afford it you could even have a trackable loved one. You couldn't see them with the naked eye, but a chart was issued to you and you could know roughly what part of the sky they moved. Every day and night.

Then the light changed.

blind.

I walk with the boy around the block a couple times. We were present when Chris started atomizing. If he made a virus, if that's even possible, then there's no telling what it can do when it's out on its own. Probably nothing. But I just had a stroke so not gonna take any chances.

The rain is lighter today. Some fog. Air feels cool on the skin. This makes the kid and I feel pretty good walking the sidewalks. He doesn't know why we're doing this. He just wants this to not ever stop. I look to my side. Light blond hair. Still clean from the hose. I find myself thinking he must be a pretty good kid, but really, I have no way of knowing. So far, he's just *other*. We round the block for the fifth time and no symptoms. I touch his forehead. Cool. No cough. No seeping blood.

THE *n*-BODY PROBLEM

There's a car in Paula and Petra's driveway. The boy and I peer in as we pass. The front door crashes open. Two teenage boys leap from the porch. We startle them and they fall onto the lawn laughing and rolling. My hand goes over the boy's face. We don't move until the teens pick themselves up. One punches the other in the nuts, sending him back down.

The kid and I advance to the steps. Trick or treat. The teenagers have killed Paula and Petra. I find Paula in the bathtub, underwater. They probably stood on her. A scum of body fluids ring the tub. An eyeball bobs in the rusty water. They used her as a trampoline for a good long while. Can't find Petra at first. The kid follows me from room to room. No emotion or sounds from him. Petra has been hanged. A rope tied to the rail on the landing leads to her. They tied her then tossed her over. No big signs of struggle. They appear to have not fought too hard against these events. Petra has started to move. I'll leave her there for now. Once on the ground they start travelling. Their skin pulling them towards walls and doors and stairs. Paula's gonna start soon. I just shut the bathroom door. See what happens. The boy sits at the kitchen table. He's right. This is all ours now. Food.

There's apples and tomato juice in the fridge. Some roots. Ginger? I snap off some celery and pour the juice. We crunch it in silence. Salt and pepper. The sides of my tongue reach over and touch each other. My lips warm. Anorexia my ass. The kid eats, too.

I'm trying to figure it. They could have killed the ladies for no reason. It isn't shocking. It's something that happens all the time. Could be a race thing, too. That definitely happens all the time. Or—and this is a possibility that's been buzzing like a wasp since we entered the house—this was a message. For me. He knows I'm in town. And he knows where in town.

Dixon and I came up through Garrison Securities together. We supplied security for covert mining operations in countries at war. Sometimes the mining companies would start the wars, carefully creating no-go zones, then mining them. And we provided safety for them in the most brutal terms. And this was before the dead got in the way. We had some horrible times, me and Dixon. We were the worst you could ever know. When it was over, we headed home and looked for work. I got into this, what I do now. Bounty hunting, really. Kill one guy to save a lot of people. Move on. I have killed forty-two Sellers. Never capture.

Dixon's a Seller. And a sadist. I've come into the towns he's done. Seen things I'll never shake. His preferred method is to collect everyone in some central part of town, then have them all hold stripped cable. Like blind people on a field trip. Then he declares to God the rightness and glory of it all and he throws the switch. It takes a while to fully kill everyone, but Dixon's smart, he doesn't use an alternating current. No one who's latched on can let go.

Then he starts to play. He drags bodies around the town, posing them, living with them for a week or two. Even fucking some of them. He deliberately works with words like obscenity and abomination in mind. That's the fate of this town. I can feel it. That's what she meant when she said she'd never find Chris if he died. If they died too far apart, they'd get hung out there in different neighbourhoods. This town is preparing to go as one.

X and I sit on the couch with a fresh plate of celery and a jug of ice water. Celery's good for blood pressure, but really not that safe to affirm old body facts. I have a lump inside my mouth below the bottom lip. It's a hard one. Fast-growing. Doesn't taste like cancer. I'm sure there's scissors in the house just in case. We can hear a continuous cricket of squeaks from the bathtub upstairs. Petra. Paula dances on the rope silently. I should check what the pick-up protocols are in this town. X and I are gonna watch some news. Haven't done that in a very long time.

the news.

The news is a long list of services available in Toronto. Food Banks. Shelters. Some work available. Not much. Daycare places. Places to take babies. Leave babies. The wave of rape that ended a year ago has yielded a baby boom. Generation Rape. The last, probably. The babies are either abandoned or fought over. Some folks love the rape babies and some hate them. Pediatrics is the only branch of medicine, the only hospital department, that still deals in old body. A few months back a visible part of the female population was pregnant. I think that, as much as anything, sank us. We became horrible to each other. The species is dying of shame.

A commercial comes on for WasteCorp. Lot of sunshine in these ads. Time lapse photography of yellow tulips becoming vertical in yellow light. Robins hooping straw on a backyard tool shelf. It's easy to hate these commercials and reasonable to do so, but there's no mistaking the way they make you feel. The TV becomes a full-spectrum light box for thirty seconds and people crane in, like basking dandelions. The lump in my mouth has changed a bit. It's a fat disc now. I picture myself turning scissors this way and that trying to feel my way to the first snips. Or do I carve an X in the chin and draw the thing out with pliers? Not worth thinking about. I'll know what to do when I do it.

News story about the thickening lattice. It's an interesting feature of orbit. Was a selling point for a while. The bodies orbit in layers, or skins as they're called, and when the skins get too deep, I think the number was 30,000 or so, then the innermost skin starts to breakdown. This was supposed to insure that the structure wouldn't become too dense or too thick. Never really worked. Whatever architecture's going on up there is evolving on its own. The other feature of the peel was that bodies would re-enter the atmosphere in a controlled way. They would burn in the sky and enter the thin stratosphere as ash. We would be able to see this at sunset. It would be natural. It would be poetry. Except it doesn't always happen like that. Some years there's no peel at all. The lattice becomes tighter. The light more fragile.

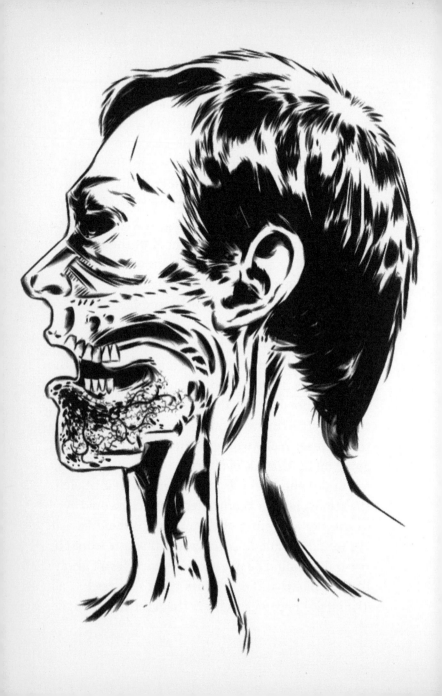

Life on earth, with no outward sign of apocalypse, is suspended by despair.

There's a story on the news about a major event over India. It's the kind of peel we see more these days. Millions of bodies at once. A massive inverted volcano in the sky over Mumbai. A funnel of hot ash and charnel debris hits the city and chokes it out. Thousands can die in these events. Their lungs fill with blood and their skin burns under accumulating death paste. WasteCorp moves in quick. The dead are conveyed. Everything starts again. It is unusual to see this actually on the news. Usually they show the inverted cone and the fierce pyroclastic ring and it's sold as a wonder, as a stunning phenomena. A murmuration of the dead. The images they're showing now, of people lying down in the streets, is rare to see. Reminds me of the term "first responders." Not many of those around anymore.

The news ends and I notice X hasn't eaten anything. It occurs to me that he isn't all that different than the dead. His movements are a little more purposeful, sure, but he doesn't speak, doesn't act on his own. I wonder what's in this kid. Honestly, he could be extremely minimal. An imitation of the new dead. I wonder if that's not a pretty good survival strategy. No thought, no danger. A reboot of Barnaby Jones on the TV. Columbian. Starring Jose Marins.

"What's this shit?"

I'm trying to see if X is there or not. He just stares.

"There's a guy after us. Old friend. He's gonna want to kill us."

Nothing.

"We're gonna have to sleep on the roof. Safest place."

X reaches over and grabs a stick of celery. He returns the hand to his lap. No eating. He's telling me not to talk to him.

I've been alone for my whole life, but this is a bit much.

dixon.

My mind has wandered. I have come to believe that I have Barrett's Syndrome or possibly esophageal cancer. When I swallow it's like my throat is too dry to complete the task. There's a constriction at the base. A burr beneath my collar bone. A bleeding white cluster of throat tubers. Voles scuttling through thin tunnels. Honeycomb tongue. It's probably because I spoke for the first time in a while. It felt unnatural. It triggered the picture. My serotonin syndrome has advanced alarmingly. I definitely have colonized stem cells. Neurotransmitter flower boxes. I need to inventory. I need to find items I can organize. I turn the TV off. It may well be giving me advanced throat cancer. I need a good honest list.

It's not enough to do things. Doing things makes thought slide, gives way to automatic images, unbidden connection. The only way to reset is deliberate lists. Mental lists. X has kicked his shoes off. There are no sores or scars or marks on his feet. A little surprising. The inflated tissue at the base of my throat makes me think of those hemorrhoid rings you sit on. There are no lists. I can't just make a list of everything. You can't just count. You can't just point. Lists stop linear chains and prevent atomization. No dictionarying. Lists take the outside and stack it inside. Lists are like chemotherapy. Chop the fear from the image. Shrink the new body. Cease evolution. I need a list that can't be ignored. That isn't inconsequential. I need a list with its own gravitational field.

Dixon.

Here is a list of the things he is known to have done with the bodies in the towns. Dixon sewed seventy-nine people together in a fountain: testicles to vaginas, testicles to tongues, testicles to eyes, testicles to anus, testicles to testicles, testicles to penis, testicles to breast, testicles to removed liver, testicle to small intestine, testicle to exposed brain, testicle to open throat, testicle to stomach lining, testicle to bone fragments, testicle to cheek, testicle to fontanel, testicle to arch, testicle to navel, testicle to bladder, testicle to eyelid, testicle to lung cancer, testicle to parotid gland, testicle to frog, testicle to windpipe.

Also involving the same seventy-nine people: vaginas to vaginas, vaginas to tongues, vaginas to eyes, vaginas to anus, vaginas to penis, vaginas to breast, vaginas to removed liver, vagina to small intestine, vagina to exposed brain, vagina to open throat, vagina to stomach lining, vagina to bone fragments, vagina to cheek, vagina to fontenal, vagina to arch, vagina to navel, vagina to bladder, vagina to eyelid, vagina to lung cancer, vagina to parotid gland, vagina to frog, vagina to windpipe.

Dixon removed his shoes and jumped across the tense, agitated surface like a kid in a bouncy castle.

Dixon tied several hundred people to a fence along the highway then drove at speed beside them with a bat held tight in the window. Dixon managed to hit most of the heads, launching bone and brains into the cows.

Dixon made a hood from the eviscerated body of an eight-month-old baby. The hood moves magically. Fingers tickling his temples. Small feet clenching on his shoulders.

Dixon made sunglasses out of the sphincters of twins. The tiny apertures working like slits to reduce brightness. Unnecessary since we have been able to stare directly into the sun for over eight years now.

Dixon has made a practise of necrophilia and his list of partners numbers in the thousands. Dixon has sex with several on a typical day.

Dixon has ejaculated into vaginas. Into anuses. Into mouths. Into eyes. Into cuts opened on every imaginable part of the body—throats, ribs, bellies, etc. Dixon has also ejaculated into brains, testicles, spines. Dixon has ejaculated inside the oldest and the youngest females. The oldest and the youngest males. Dixon has attempted to ejaculate on those merely stunned by electrocution and has had to kill the person manually in order to ejaculate. Dixon has ejaculated wearing a cored penis on his own penis. Noting the cored penis moves on its own like a worm shroud. Dixon has ejaculated in the hole left by a severed penis. It is impossible to finish this list as it is always longer than one imagines. Ejaculations involved penetration where practical.

Dixon drained the blood from fifty-four people into a dry swimming pool. Dixon studied the eddies and currents as they changed over days. Eventually, Dixon bathed in it and marvelled at the live blood and how its caresses varied endlessly.

Dixon has boiled an older woman's head and removed, cubed, and eaten the brain.

Dixon, on a particularly random moonlit night, ran down the line taking single bites from faces. He then joined the corpses by hooking fingers into the holes.

Dixon has dropped people from the tops of bridges, tall buildings, hydro towers, waterfalls, churches, trees, and grain silos.

Dixon has lined up hundreds of naked people in chairs on a road then driven a pick-up into them at 160 km/h. He has done this numerous times. His record is seventy-eight people—that's how many bodies it took to stop the vehicle.

Dixon has slept on a woman whom he thought he knew.

Dixon has skinned many dozens and taken pictures.

Dixon removed the testicles from eleven scrotums and inserted them through deep slits into the body of a heavy man, like cloves of garlic in a turning pig carcass. Dixon cooked him, but only ate the testicles, which he tore out with a rake. Dixon noted that cooking someone only slows movement and that when it cools the skin hardens like a carapace and only the fatty tissue beneath can move.

Dixon has put an unborn into a newborn into a toddler into a child into a teenager into a medium-sized woman into a medium-sized man into a large woman into a large man into an obese woman into an obese man and bound the latter in bailer twine. He noted the movement inside was almost undetectable but the sounds coming from the layers were complex and loud.

This is a partial list. I hate everything he has done since becoming a Seller.

bright spots.

I find about twelve cedar planks in the garage. Sit and lift them to my nose one at a time, inhaling hungrily. These are old cedar, maybe even predating the orbit. Real sunlight made them. The effect is gorgeous.

I am lifted into memories I've never had. Runnning down a dock and leaping into cold water. On a high ladder hanging a birdhouse. Lying in the bottom of a boat.

X interrupts.

"What's up?"

X stands. I bet he can't be alone.

"Check out this wood. Want to build something?"

X hops down the step into the garage. I nod. He has just distinguished himself from the dead. The dead don't hop. I give him the upturned bucket I'm sitting on and look at the narrow worktable. The smell of spruce. Faint though.

"Let's build something, man."

I turn to X sitting on the bucket. He is sniffing the cedar. His eyes are closed. It's an instinctive thing to do, I guess. A natural hunger.

"Ok. That's fine with me."

I sit on the floor beside him and lift a plank to my nose.

X opens his eyes and sees me pushing my face into the wood. X laughs.

This makes my stomach roll over. It's like an overly rich meal. I try to keep from throwing up. This is too good to lose.

It isn't easy getting out on the roof, let alone dragging what we need up there. I find a rope ladder in an upstairs closet. It's part of a emergency fire escape kit. Flashlight and water and a blanket. I lean out a top floor window and hammer the ladder to the facia board. A bit startled to see a school bus stop at a house near the corner. A child leaves his mother at the end of the driveway and boards the bus. It's easy to forget that everyone's situation is different. Who knows what goes on in that house. On that bus. Or the school. I peer back through the window. X hasn't seen it.

We hand-ferry two sleeping bags and pillows up to the roof. And some sheets to hold us in. We'll do this at the back of the roof so we can't be seen. It's a pretty simple, crude rig, the only drawback being the last time I did this was with Dixon in Daychopan about twenty-one years ago. Dix won't think of it. We lay the bags and pillows out, then the sheets across. We nail the edges like a canvas stretched in a frame. X has had noticeably more life since the cedar and that's good. I need the hands. Thought I might.

We slip down into the bags and test the strength. It's a steep roof so my body pulls pretty good, but I put the roofing nails in a tight stitch patter. Should hold. It's not raining, which is rare and lucky, but that could change. We'll be sleeping in rainwater barrels if it does. X is swallowed by his rig. I have to help him up. I show him how to keep his arms over and the bag from under his armpits to clip himself in. He follows instruction well. Damn cedar is helping us both, I think. The sun will go down soon. We lie still and look up at the sky.

The sky.

I stare into the sun sitting low. You can't see them. One billion obstructions moving invisibly across the setting sun. There is usually cloud cover, but not tonight. The sky is wide and clear. I study it, as everybody does, for its difference. There is a black sparkle in the sun's corona. That's been there for a few years. The blue turns green around the horizon. And there's a pink flicker midway up. Fancy cocktail colours. Strawberry, lime, apple, blue Curaçao. Solid syrupy light. You feel that it must be sticky to touch. The thin clouds stuck like cotton candy to a wall. That might be why it's overcast so often. The cloud canopy gets snagged to the tacky sky above. There is my stroke egg, like a too-close planet. Looks like it belongs up there. These colours appear at sunset. During the day the blue is different only because you imagine it must be.

I check X. Still clipped in. He isn't looking up. I reach across and touch his face. It's warm. There is some warmth coming from the sun still. Some radiation sneaking through. Pieces of the spectrum, the vitamins in fault lines and thin spots. Reminds me that I forgot to take my vitamin D drops. Can't miss those. Makes your autoimmune go crazy if you do. MS. Lupus. Strange allergies. My arm turned to bloody rubble once, after a mosquito bite. Took months of Benadryl, which had its own knockoff effects. The arm is still grey. X looks at me. Or it's not the sun. It's a fever. Maybe he'll die up here, in the next few hours.

"You think we'll get any sleep tonight?"

X looks at me, into my eyes. He nods. The effect on me is powerful and sudden. He strokes the back of my neck while I sob. It's something I never feel. I am grieving for my species. I am grieving for everyone. It is an emotion with no real history and it shatters you when it comes. I love people. I want to be one again. But this will never ever happen. X is pushing a water bottle to my mouth. He doesn't want me to cry all the water from my body. I drink. I can't cry and drink at the same time. I hand the water back to X. Thank Christ that doesn't happen very often. Some people get started and never stop. Not me. I have a cold side. Smooth and silent and cold. I try to restore it. The water rolls down the cold stones stacked in my chest.

"Thanks. Sorry."

X has turned his head. He doesn't want to hurt me again. Irony is I feel my chest shake at the thought of him protecting me.

Car door slam. From the driveway. Dixon.

I place my hand firmly on X and he turns. I put my finger to my lips. Like he's gonna talk. The front door bangs closed. X and I lie perfectly still. Dixon will walk the house. He'll see Petra dancing on the rope. Paula squirming under water. Did I leave stalk ends on the counter? Will he pick up and check the wilt of celery? Know the time when it was cut? After the hanging and the stomping? Will he figure this out? If he does he'll know where I am. He'll check the room upstairs. The emergency kit on the floor. Did we close the window? He'll see the ladder.

I listen. I test the sheets. We are butterflies pinned to matte board. Already dead. Embalmed. He'll torture us lying here before he kills us. He wants me to suffer more than anything. He wants me to beg for my life.

Bang. Front door. Wait. Clunk. Car door. The engine whines.

I exhale. He has come and gone. He lost my trail. He forgot about our roof trick. X senses that I have relaxed and turns to me. I smile. It's not bad. It doesn't hurt. He smiles back. I want to take this now. I put my hand on his head and he pushes it against my palm. I feel we are together. If we die up here tonight, of typhus or AIDS or madness or the flu, we will die having seen each other. And then, who knows? Maybe we'll hang up there in the same spot and feel that sun for the first time. See the earth. This is a happiness, but I'm not stupid. It's just as dangerous as a sadness. Happiness removes suppression. It makes you want to die. I feel heat against my back.

A pigtail of black smoke runs across the eaves. Dixon knows exactly where I am. He has set the house on fire. He'll have used an accelerant. I push up and feel flop sweat on my chest. I pull at the roofing nails and the sheet tears. X is turning in his bag unable to free himself. My first impulse is to leave him to die. He's going to hold me back, get us both killed. Then I remember and pull his sheet with two fists. Flames appear around one edge then another. The roof will drop soon. It will fold around us any moment. X runs to the peak, but that's where the fire will punch through first. I throw myself flat and grab his ankle. He drops and slides uncontrollably down the steep pitch. X disappears into a high funnel of flame.

I have nothing left to do but follow.

There is no air in my lungs. There is no sound in my ears. I can smell my body burning. Nothing is visible but the tiny stroke egg and the anamorphic line. And heat. I am hung before the sun.

i am not hung before the sun.

X is putting me out with a garden hose. I can see him naked in the alley covered in his mother's shit, trying to get away from the icy water. I feel we are amazing friends. In the shock, entire years of our adventure passes through me.

The time we stayed with that widow in a shack by the pond. How we buried her kin for her.

The time we hunted deer on the escarpment and saw a lynx. And a hognose snake. Yes! And we met other hunters at the top. They were drinking and we started drinking and shooting our rifles at fungus on a birch tree.

The time we rushed to the water's edge. The time we saw the egret. The massive shell of a roadside turtle. Its head was the size of a hockey helmet.

We had trouble one winter living in an abandoned blind. It was a bad idea. You can't tell how cold it's going to get. How high the snow will drift. And the wind. Remember those nights. We slept with our fingers in our ears.

I can feel where I am but I can't be there. I have no heart and no mind. No body. I am tiny scales on the hunched back of a great golden carp. Each scale like a tiny screen that pulls at me with story. Light pulls me into the fish's side. I am in the care of curled carp. Minnows. Waterborne lint. I am its telescopic mouth. Barbels. Bluegills.

Blue. Blue water. Blue sky.

in the unlikely event that i am writing please read this.

We are in a shed. Probably still on the property. I am wrapped in a mulch bag from a lawn tractor.

"Why are we hiding?"

That was X. I try to talk but my throat is closed around a cancer in my thyroid. This is why I am sick.

"I don't fucking get it," X says, turns to me. He has a cloth and he stuffs it in my mouth. Cold water fills the spaces between my teeth.

"Suck on that. We leave here soon."

I obey. I feel a sharp line across my upper stomach. Duodenitits. Esophagitis. Not fatal things on their own but they are never on their own.

X is watching me and I close my eyes. I lay my hands on my belly. It feels distended, wobbly. There are many reasons why this could be happening. Daylight penetrates my eyelids.

"Here. See if you need anything," he says.

I look down at a small greasy box X has placed at my side. I expect to see machine parts and am surprised by pill bottles of various size. Lean to my side. The belly pulls down and out.

I pull one. Effexor. Another. Xanax. Others. Mostly SSRIs and benzo. This shit speeds up the receptor ganglia in stems. This shit is shit. This is why doctors don't see us anymore. I pull the cloth from my mouth.

"Where'd this come from?"

X doesn't answer. He stands by the shed door.

"X! Hey! Where'd this shit come from?"

X turns.

"That's not my name."

I sit and my middle doesn't fold in, it falls.

"What is this?"

X crouches beside me. He has a silver spike, snapped off the bottom of a sprinkler. "Do you think it's crazy out there?"

I rattle the box. He's been taking these. The short-term effect is always diminished symptoms. Long term, it's all syndrome.

"Why am I looking in a box of shit?"

"I broke into a few houses. Took whatever I could remember my mom taking. She said it kept her alive."

That means some people died. You can't just stop taking this stuff. Not anymore. I did. I had to taper down to grains. Over months. I still have syndrome, but I know I bought some time ditching these. Now I take oils. Moderates the immune system responses. That's the best. Evening primrose. Flax seed. Fish oil. And Vitamin D. Fuck with brain chemistry and you die soon.

"Throw this out. This is bad fuel. Here."

I drag my bag off my shoulder and dump the oils and D.

"I'll share these."

X looks sceptical.

"But my Mom—"

"Your Mom dissolved in her own shit."

X gives me a look. His hand around that spike. I return the look. I'm not trying to be an asshole. He loosens. Thinks. That's right. You listen.

"If you're gonna steal, steal things we can use. Memorize these labels. This stuff we're gonna need."

He lowers his head and examines the cod liver oil.

"How bad do you think it is out there?" X nods to the light. The SSRIs and benzos have given him swagger.

"I don't know, man. Probably bad. Put down the spike."

X holds it firm and raises a cocky eyebrow—you sure about that?

"Please."

I reach over and hold the back of his hand. The spike falls.

"Okay," he says. "Why are we hiding? What are we doing?"

Fuck. Those damn pills sure jack up the motivation.

"How old are you?"

"I think I'm around thirteen."

I nod. A little older than I first thought. But it's feasible. Especially now that he's accelerated his gangster puberty.

"Okay. I have to make a decision, X."

"My name is Y."

"Y."

I sit up farther. My belly prevents my knees from rising.

"I have to decide whether I bring you along or whether I put you down."

Y is crushed by this. Glassy eyes start to fill.

"Not put you down. Not really. Listen. This is my work. I'm working. And if I haul you along with me you have to understand the job and you have to let me be your boss. I mean your total boss."

Y thinks. He picks up the spike and taps it on the tip of his sneakers. He speaks without looking up.

"What's the job."

"Kill a guy."

He loves that.

"Who?"

"A guy, I said."

Y nods, like he thinks this sounds doable. He's all bluff. I could knock his lights out so easy.

"When?"

"When? I don't know when."

Y bites his lip. Reasonable, he thinks. That's reasonable.

"The guy who burned the house out from under us," I say.

Y's eyes widen, darken. There's real ugly in a child on SSRIs and benzos.

"Let's kill that fuckin' guy, then."

to learn what's going on.

Things get moving pretty early in this town. Streets get swept. The message box gets changed out in front of the Evangelical Church to "He is Risen." I recognize Russel with the letters. I wave. He looks. The sky is covered again. Low cloud. Probably best. I'm in a low-intensity mood. High school kids are out. Golden Apple is open for breakfast. Y is walking just back a bit, studying the signs of things. He catches up.

"It's not really bad out here."

He's relieved. That's better, tough guy.

"Nope. I guess it ain't."

People live here. That's what I see. Husband and wife rolling wheelbarrows into place outside the Home Hardware. You can't tell what you're looking at. I'm pretty sure these people are talking about suicide. Just not to me.

"Let's eat some food."

Golden Apple is all pine booths and blond wainscoting. Heavy lacquer. Three old guys in overalls and tractor caps stop talking when we walk past. I almost say hello.

Y orders himself breakfast. Three eggs. Sausage. Bacon. Home fries. Rye toast. Large orange juice. I remember that. The pills give you a new appetite. For a while. I order coffee and a single scrambled egg. Line up the oils. My side is sore where I hit the ground. My belly has swollen a bit more in the last fifteen minutes or so. Y has frown lines. He's ageing. Something's up there.

"You get hurt at all?"

Kid's light. Probably hit the ground like a snowflake. He dismisses the question. My eggs come first. The waitress has a pine look to her. Knotty and yellow. Cigarettes. Why not?

"We need a base."

Thought he'd like that.

"Fuckin' right we do."

I knock some ketchup on the plate.

"Don't swear all the time. I don't."

I give and I can take away. He accepts.

"There any other B and Bs in town?" I ask.

"Nope. Only one."

"And now that's up in smoke."

"I forgot to check," Y says. "Could see the ladies in there?"

Y leans back as his plate lands.

"That is one horrific thing to see," I say.

"What?"

"When they get scrambled up in a fire like that. They get mixed into everything. Everything moves. You gotta look closely to see it. Give you nightmares."

He's eating fast. I push the oils closer to him. I'm worried about withdrawal.

"How long was I out?" I ask.

"Two days."

That's not bad. He'll feel it but it won't kill him. I gotta figure out why my stomach is getting larger.

"Did fire trucks come?"

"Nope. I think the guy next door was hosing down his roof in case it spread."

One of the old guys is staring at us. He's wondering what the fuck. I glance at Y. He's downing the oils now.

"People know you're not my son."

Y is having trouble with the omega. He'll get used to it.

"I'm your uncle."

Y accepts, swallowing. "This about the Seller in town?"

"What about the Seller in town?"

"I don't know much. Mom took me to the car a couple days after he showed."

"Yeah. It's about the Seller."

"Okay. Well. His name is Art something."

"No, it ain't, but whatever."

"He was at the soccer field a lot. That's all I know. People seemed to know he was a Seller and some liked it."

"Yeah. That's where he started. By now he's established a place. He's holding meetings."

Teenage mom with a rape baby sits in the booth behind us. You can bet she's onside with the Seller by now. You can tell cause she likes her baby. Talks to it. She wouldn't do that if she thought they had long to live.

"Time to go," I say. We grab our shit and head out.

It's raining again. I prefer that. Hide the damn sky so I can think.

"Can I ask you a question?"

I'm torn about my decision to cut the kid off. There is an upside to having him focused like this. Who knows what he'll be like? I decide to ditch him if he reverts too much.

"This is a job, right?"

"Yeah. That's what I said."

"Who hired you?"

Is there harm in answering that?

"School board."

Y laughs. He can laugh at that. It's pretty funny. Bunch of administrative educators hiring a hit man. Truth is, they are legally obliged to get a Hunter if they think a Seller has been in contact with anyone on school property.

"This Seller's a sick one. He'll start hitting people who don't climb on."

"Hitting?"

"Torture relatives. Drug people. Kill some. School board's probably bought already."

Another teenage mom with a rape baby. Man, you can see what this place was like a year ago. She's happy, too. Dixon.

"He's done thousands at a time. All singing the same song. He doesn't really like to hurt them when they live."

I salute the young mom. Who the fuck knows why.

"Anyway. He's not somebody you wanna die around."

We're coming to the end of Main Street. Man, these towns are small. Hard to hide.

"Look, I got a feeling he's closed on a lot of people. We gotta be careful. Can't buy much. Can't talk too much. Can't stay anywhere anyone knows. Is there a park?"

"Down the alley between Ole Pizza and the chocolate store."

"Ok. Let's go live in the trees."

I pull out a pad.

"Here's what you need to steal. Meet me in the park."

I write: Razor. Soap. Shampoo. Large tub of vaseline.

"Don't buy it. Steal it."

Probably be better if I had one of those rape-baby moms. Bet they shoplift all day.

the trees by the stream in the park behind the chocolate store.

I only make it halfway through the alley and have to lean against the brick. There is a sharp pain in my stomach. And it's distended now to the point where it handicaps me. I push a hand in. Very soft. Like it's full of water. I can feel a corner of the liver is hardened. Cirrhosis? Maybe. Too much anxiety about meds. Too much looking at the sky. This could be big. All my pushing has made me need to shit. I drop my pants and slide my back down the wall. It comes out as water. Like a tap I turn on under my nuts. I bounce over as it moves around my feet. There's more. Maybe that's it. Maybe it's irritable bowel. I watch the dark leafy fluid run down the alley. If there's blood then I am fucked. Crohn's disease would explain the pain.

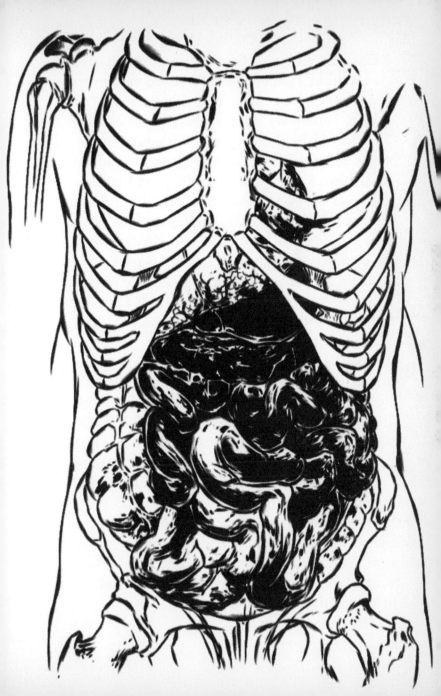

Longitudinal ulcer in the large intestine. Inflamed, even morbid, splenetic plicture. Could explain the hard liver. Spleen might be going up too. What a mess. I study my shit for blood. So far nothing. What would be the outcome? Without steroids I might bleed to death. God, I regret dumping all those benzos now. Sometimes they can be magic. Feel good and everything falls back in line. I need a full spectrum light too. I finally stop shitting. I close my eyes and try to recall the scent of cedar, but all I'm getting is the bland filth rolling down this alley. I pull up my pants. The fabric fuses to my ass and wicks the muck up. Did he say there was a stream? Gotta be. Gotta move.

I launch off the wall and fall down. My palms in shit. No blood. I crawl to the dry wall. A loud fart that opens my body from asshole to mouth. I wonder if there were any opioids in that box. Fuck. That'd be great. Shut the digestive system down like it had a switch. Hard as hell to live clean. Not so sure it's the best idea anymore. It feels like something is hanging off me. I can feel gravity on my belly. I stand. My belly is bigger. This is in my abdominal cavity. This isn't Crohn's or IBS. This could be far worse. Definitely cancer. And lots. I'm cascading here. I think I know what it is. I'm afraid to say. Sometimes accepting contains it and sometimes it just blows the shit right up.

"Holy shit. Are you okay?"

I sit on the ground and pull out my pad.

"Go back to the shed. Check the box for these."

I write: Diazepam. Lorazepam. Xanax. Tylenol 3. Fentanyl. Oxicontin.

"'But, I thought . . .'"

"This is an emergency. Emergencies are different. Don't bring back anything but these."

He drops a razor, soap, shampoo, and a huge tub of Vaseline on the ground. Grabs the list and runs. I'm scaring the hell out of this kid. He does not like it when grownups shit themselves.

I call out after him.

"I'll be in the goddam river!"

Y turns the corner.

"Hey! Is there a river?"

It's not quite a river. A stream. A crick. A mom nursing by the slide. A couple small bridges. Some trees. Big willows. Back up there there's poplar. Birch. Manitoba maple. Lots of scrub. Don't know what I was picturing but this ain't it. Can't live in a fuckin' birch tree.

I salute the mom from a distance. It's something I've picked up. Saluting teen moms with rape babies. The banks are landscaped and have good dropped shoulders so I can sit out of sight. I kick off my shoes and work the pants down. Just gonna lay all this under rocks and rub myself on the grass like a dog. There is strain on my rib cage. My lungs are pulling shallow. Pain hits again. Cold, waxy sweat rubs off solid in the grass. I am really fucking sick now. Hands and feet buzzing. Peripheral neuropathy. Feel like heavy socks and gloves. Could be unrelated. Who knows? If this is a cascade then I could have minutes. Shit.

I lie still on my side. I can feel some light on my naked body. Bad light is still bad light. I should cover up, but I'm dying.

"Shit! Shit! Hey! Talk to me!"

That's Y. I must have drifted off. I'm shivering. He sits me up. I can't stop shaking. There's shit soaked into the grass around me. White vomit on my arm.

"What do you want? What do you want?"

The stroke egg is strobing. Y shoves the box into my hands. He brought everything. I thought I said . . .

"Just take something!"

Hard to read. My eyes feel dry and sticky.

"Oxycontin."

Y flips the bottles around in the box.

"Here! Here! How many?"

I can feel a thick python separate my lungs.

"Six."

I eat them like peanuts. Make a paste. Hold it sublingually. That's the way. By the time it's in my throat I can feel my toes curl a bit. A warmth in my eyes. A harmonica.

"What else? What else?"

"Diazepam."

Y digs.

"Nope. None."

"Shit. Ok. Lorazepam."

Y pulls out a long thin bottle.

"They 1s or 2s?"

Read it, pal. Read.

"2."

"Ok. Then four."

I hold them under my tongue till they disappear. Lorazepam leaves the system after about eight hours. They're tougher in large doses than diazepam, which sits in you for a good long while. My arms turn to pillows. My shoulders into smooth falling sacs. I close my eyes. I greet the egg. It is my old friend. No one has seen you. No one knows what you are. You are mine.

"Better?"

I keep my eyes closed and reach out to lay a hand on the grass near Y. I can hear water moving. He's getting my clothes. Doesn't like to see his uncle naked in the park.

"I'm sorry. These are wet."

They are. I move my head so that the egg is in my shoe. Not sure why. I salute Y.

"Get dressed," Y says.

I fall asleep for a second. "Okay. Help me."

Y sits me up and drops the icy shirt over my head. It's good. I wake.

"I found something else. Look."

I drag the denim up my thighs and pinch the button closed.

"Look."

A portable full-spectrum lamp. I haven't seen one of these in a long time. Very expensive.

"It was in our trunk. My dad bought it for my mom for her birthday."

I turn it on. Bright. Good batteries. Holy shit.

"My dad had money. He owned the quarry."

I hold the light up to my face. Y keeps talking.

"What's wrong with your stomach? It's huge."

I can't answer. The light and the pills are profound in me. It's like the cells are giddy. Everything is turning in every direction. There is so much good.

"My mom's gone."

That's good. Made the pick-up.

"She'll be up there."

I grunt. I feel freshly split cedar in my marrow. Dark rich hardwood in my veins.

"We could clean up the car."

Nope.

"I mean. It's a car."

Not a chance.

"How you feel now?"

I pass Y the spectrum.

"Much better. Here. Take a turn. Five minutes."

I have stopped the cascade. Not solved the problem but at least I won't die in the park this morning.

"Thanks. Your belly is still big."

It is. Not getting bigger any more. But if this is what I think it is then it's left me a little present. Y looks thirty. Teen mom appears behind Y.

"What are you guys doing?"

She takes it in. She turns, runs.

"Shit."

Y stands to see where she goes.

"What?"

"We just lost an advantage."

Y looks like he's going to run after her.

"Why?"

"Your Seller knows we're still alive."

Y takes a step back. Attaboy.

"Let her go. Can't go around killing moms in the park."

I try to stand. There is pain but it's not from anything advancing. It's from the volume in my abdomen. I can walk.

"Let's go find a sharp knife. I'm gonna need you to cut me open."

can a toaster cry?

I remember Barack Obama. I remember terrorism. Higgs-Boson. I remember a cure for AIDS. Charity walks for breast cancer. I remember when they told us to sit up straight at computers. To clench and unclench our buttocks while we sat. Guns going off. *Iron Man 4*. It's strange that you stop thinking about things. Even further back. I remember Iggy Pop. Safe havens in Bosnia. Me as a teenager. I didn't really know it at the time but there was nothing to it. It's not that things fade in time. It's that they were never really there at all. All of it. Light as birthday cards. Gone.We are at the loading dock behind the hardware store. Y has snuck in to steal a blade. Narcotics have encased my bowels in concrete. It's better than collapsing in shit, but it hurts. It's hard to move freely.

What I think I have is . . . it's a cancer that coats organs in the abdominal cavity. Doesn't enter the lymphatic system. Not for a while. I hope it hasn't anyway. It starts like a coating on the spleen. A woman's shawl. And it triggers peritoneal fluid to build up. Ascites. The bells thicken and the cancer cells are released into the fluid-like spores from a bumped fungus. They drape the liver. They drape the colon. The stomach lining. The fluid accommodates this by separating the packed bodies. Creating living space for itself. And the more this cancer silt builds, the thicker and heavier the mucous becomes. Eventually the spleen sloughs off its new deadly skin and releases it as a transparent tube, a hovering jellyfish in a dark thick sea. It is a new part of you. It is a distinct creature looking to live in you. Your body recognizes it. Even in the insensate mash of glue and fatted lungs, it is awake to this new thing, the birth of this tube. And your body trusts its origin. It is a child of the spleen. It is your tissue. It is splendid and structured and hungry. So the body feeds it. That's how you die. Your body is so desperate that this tube survive that it takes all the blood and oxygen away from what you really are and feeds this new child. This lovely tube-shaped wonder. It flattens and expands and floats. It is free. It is alone in you. It is wonderful. And then you die. Not of cancer. The cancer is just starlight. The cancer

is a maker. You die of a neglected liver. Abandoned to necrotize like an old city. You are ruins.

So I'm cutting it out. I'm waiting for Y. I look around for a place to do this. I can't walk far. I walk bowlegged to a derelict car by the dumpster. I will sit with my feet on the ground and my belly hanging. That way when we cut the base it'll drain straight away. The cut will have to be big enough for his hand to get in. He's going to have to pull this out.

Y rolls across the loading dock and drops, crouched, on the dirt. He has something in his hand. Before I look I put four oxys and a couple Lorazapam under my tongue. Liver spot on his hand.

"Here."

Y holds out a box cutter. Still in the package. Not sure what I was expecting, but I guess nothing's gonna be great.

"Okay."

Y bites it open and removes the knife. He pushes the small triangular blade out.

"Is this clean?" I take the knife and smell it.

"Factory fresh. You ready?"

I take my shirt off and push my stomach down closer to the ground.

"Now? Here?"

I hand him back the cutter. "No time like now."

He takes the knife.

"Is this going to kill you?'

86

He wants to know what happens to him.

"Maybe."

We look at each other for long moment. I'm supposed to say something.

"If I die, you have to leave town."

Sorry, kid. That's all I got. There's not much else, believe me.

"You ready?"

He's holding the cutter like it might jump outta his hand. Good grip.

"Ok. We'll go easy here. Nothing fast or too big."

I point to the base of my stomach, where it's closest to the ground.

"You wanna cut here. The full depth of that blade. Then let's see what comes out."

He looks at me expecting more.

"If I pass out, this is what I want you to do. There should be lotsa fluid. Let it drain. You can squeeze the sides of my belly to help it along. But easy! Go easy. You don't wanna pop my guts out onto the ground. Right?"

He stares.

"Right?"

C'mon. I need you in this moment. He nods.

"Say it."

"Right."

I look at the way he's holding the cutter. Not sure if there's a right way and a wrong way.

"Cut just enough to get your hand in."

He's looking at my massive white belly hanging over the gravel. He looks sick.

"Hang on. I should swallow some antibiotics. Pass the box."

There's amoxicillin and tetracycline . . . I take three of each, let them turn to paste, then swallow them.

"You'll have to flush my guts with the hose. Quick though. Like, seconds. That alone's probably gonna kill me."

Y squats in front of me. He is very pale.

"Staple it up when you're done. I don't know how aware I'm gonna be."

I tap the underside of my belly and give Y a quick shallow nod.

"Don't pull the skin. Let the blade lead the way."

He presses the point against my skin. A bright pain.

"C'mon. Get in there. That hurts."

I feel a hot throb and the piercing pain stops. He slides the knife across. It feels like fabric separating.

"Deeper, Y. You gotta reach the stomach."

He drives it in and I feel a blunt pulse until—pop. The stomach wall.

"That's it."

It feels like the claw of a cat drawing a line inside. He stops.

"What's happening?"

Y is staring down.

"Nothing. Hardly any blood even."

"Do it again. Same place."

This time I feel no pain, just a bubbling sensation in my lower back. I can hear splashing on the ground between my feet.

"Okay. Okay. Squeeze that stuff out."

Y' s forehead on my chest while he milks the mucous from my torso.

"Good enough. Go in. Stick your hand in."

I look down and see Y's hand disappear into my stomach."

"Look for it. Something loose. Squishy. Don't pull on anything attached."

Uh-oh. Okay. World of wonders. Goodbye.

EDITOR'S NOTE: The following chapter is encoded. The code however is not available for this publication and will appear in H.A.M.S. Lesson 4. The publisher's objection to this gimmick is on record.

H.A.M.S. and egg.

$\underline{m}_k$ Σ | $^3\Sigma$ (, $j\underline{m}_k\Sigma$ $j\underline{m}_k$(| ^{3}G $m_,,(\underline{m}_j$|)Σ|j K$\neq_j$ $q_k$under| ^{3} ,j=1GΣ|j, $q_k$under K$\neq_j$ $\underline{m}_k$. m_j.).,.:)
$m_j\underline{\ }\Sigma$ m_j = $q_k$under,j=1)Σ. (j)m_j, $q_j$umlautΣ m_j|, =$\underline{m}_k m_j$| ^3m_j=jΣ| ^{3}, m_j|, =| $^3\Sigma$mj=1| $^3\Sigma$. (j)
m_j, $q_j$umlautΣ)m_jGΣ K$\neq_j$| ^{3} $q_k$under) m_j|,)
m_jjΣ| ^{3}(m_jq_j. (K$\neq_j$,Σ.(|$\underline{m}_j$ (, | $q_k$underj , $q_k$under =1| ^{3} ,j| ^3q_kunder|$\underline{m}_j$,=1(j, ,$q_k$under=1)m_j,
,=1$q_j$umlaut)(j m_j ,$\underline{\ }\Sigma$j=$\underline{m}_k$ $q_k$under K$\neq_j$ m_j =$q_k$under,j=1)Σ, $q_k$under| ^{3} m_j
under$\underline{m}_kq_k$underj$q_k$under$\underline{m}_j$| ^3m_j-under$\underline{m}_k$ $q_k$underK$\neq_j$ m_j =$q_k$under,j=1)Σ. ,$q_k$under=1)m_j,
,=1$q_j$umlaut)(j m_j =$q_k$under)-under$q_k$under|Σ|j underm_j| ^{3}j $q_k$under K$\neq_j$ m_j =$q_k$under,j=1)Σ
— m_j .($\underline{m}_j$, m_j $\underline{m}_k m_j$j, m_j)m_j,$\underline{\ }$ — $j\underline{m}_k m_j$j
,$q_k$under=1 $\underline{m}_k m_j$,.Σ)m_jGΣ $q_k$under| ^{3} $j\underline{m}_k m_j$j
,$q_k$under=1 $\underline{m}_k m_j$,.Σ -under=1| ^{3}=$\underline{m}_k m_j$,ΣG m_j|G
-underΣ| ^{3},$q_k$under|m_jq_j($n\Sigma$G. ,$q_k$under=1)
m_j, | $^3\Sigma$=| $^3\Sigma$mjΣ $j\underline{m}_k\Sigma$ =| $^3\Sigma$-underΣ -under=1)-
under$\underline{\ }$(| =$q_jq_k$under.| =$q_k$under,j=1)Σ $j\underline{m}_k m_j$j
),)$q_k$underj$\underline{m}_k\Sigma$| ^{3})m_jGΣ m_j|G .$q_k$under| $^3\Sigma$;
,$q_k$under=1)m_j, | $^3\Sigma$=| $^3\Sigma$mjΣ (j, $j\underline{m}_k\Sigma$| ,Σj (j
$q_k$under| K$\neq_j$ (| $^3\Sigma$. ,Σ|G)Σ $j\underline{m}_k\Sigma$ m_j,$\underline{m}_k\Sigma$,.

shirley.

Not wanting to die is hardwired into every living thing. Part of the dynamic. You remove that and there's not much more than a couple crazy days left. I don't want to die. I know exactly what will happen when I do. I'll be up there. Right there. Less happy. Naked. In full view of the universe. No. I can't die.

I am unconscious for three weeks. No dreams. No fitful awakenings. Just an anvil-heavy black. My starless mind. My thinking started up rapidly however. I knew I was surfacing as I did, and it *was* surfacing, I could feel my arms break the top. My face pulled up. Warmth and light and buzzing.

We are in the walk-in clinic. I am on couch in a quiet room. A picture of the inner ear.

I lay my hand on my stomach. I can feel the bones

in my back. I look down, my wrists and hands sit up like mantis limbs. Thin bones and crispy yellow skin.

The door opens. Y sees me. Stops.

"You're awake. Okay. We gotta go. Now."

Y lowers me carefully into the passenger seat of a red Toyota in the clinic driveway.

I find I can't move and breathe at the same time. I have no strength to ask what is happening.

There are five bodies on the road. A heavy wire has been strung through their temples and fixed to lamp standards. They hang like blood candles.

"They're doing pick-ups starting past the Foodland. We can miss them if we stick to Warrington all the way out. They see someone alive they'll kill us and throw us in. These guys."

Y is driving. He's big for thirteen. I remember he said he was thirteen. There is grey in the bristles on his chin. An arrangement of bodies on a lawn. Each has another's genitals in their mouths. They move in small shakes.

"The Seller got everybody."

A hydro tower. There are at least a hundred people on a long rope, like fish on a stringer. There are random flips of tails and clapping gills. Blood in a bathtub dragged beneath them. The bathtub sits in a lake of blood.

"I know where he went."

I lay my thin hands on my hips. The points are

sharp. My knees are pointed.

"WasteCorp got here yesterday. They're picking up everybody. Dead, half-dead, anything. They're tossing everything in."

The sky is full of vultures and rain. That always happens. As soon as the animals realize the people are dead, they move in. Take over. Rats. Raccoons. Possum. They disappear into the corpses.

"You okay?"

Y looks at me. Impatience. I'm guessing he almost left me to die. Probably did a couple times.

"I'm not doing that again."

Y is disgusted. He has contempt. I imagine myself thanking him but can't. My brain feels dry and hot. I have crammed myself into a very small hole up there. To survive.

Y gives me a suspicious look.

"You better not be dead."

A long arm with heads nailed into its muscles reaches across the road and crumples the roof. I'm hallucinating. Carnival sounds. The feeling that I am in clown makeup. Why does delirium use such stock figures?

"You better show me you're alive or I'm rolling you out this car."

I need anti-psychotics. I need to say something. He's going to drop me into a sea of bodies. I have to say something.

"*Comme ci, comme ça.*"

"What?"

I try to make saliva.

"*Comme ci, comme ça.*"

Y Laughs.

"Really? *Comme ci, comme ça?*"

I nod.

"Well, okay. You're doing better than you look."

There is a wide hole all around me. The underside of ground. Red tree roots and broken mason jars. The snipping teeth of mice. Everything needs to dive. Get below. The bones of dogs. The fat death mask of a grub. The yellow plans of beetles and worms and a moon princess.

Goodbye.

a weeks.

There is a soft light in the clouds this morning. I swing carefully on the porch. Y is in the field. It has been weeks. I saw terrible things. I was kept alive by these jolts. These images. And Y's portable lamp. I am, for now, in old body. No syndrome. No disease being cooked up by winds in my blood. Y is heading to the house. Pail of radishes. Carrots. I am an old woman swinging on the porch. Grateful to her son. He drops the pail and wipes his brow.

"Surprised these are growing."

I look out to a copse across the field. It appears like a lead shroud. There is no green anymore. Leaves are grey and black. It gives the land a metallic look. Grass is silver. Odd behaviour in birds. They circle trees in mad spins. Small bushes take on the look of manic gyroscopes. I stop swinging and peer into the pail. Something grew anyway. Carrots look like long teeth. Radishes like filthy buttons.

"Let's eat them. We got oil and vitamin D. We're fine."

We eat inside by candlelight. The vegetables are tasteless and, worse, ugly. Y had followed Dixon out of town while I was out. He was going back and forth between two towns. Y thinks this second town is his next target. I have to call it in to the school board. I can't afford to be feral. This is my job. I want to get paid. I want to get out.

"I'm calling the school board after dinner."

Y doesn't react to this. He pulls a thong of carrot from the back of his throat. He saw it all back there. All of Dixon's merriment. He wants to hunt. So do I.

"Once I get clearance, we go in."

Y and I have never talked much. We stick to practical words. What we will do. What we need. A bird hits the window and drops straight down. That happens dozens of times a day. This house sits in a bed of bird carcasses.

Tonight the cloud cover is high and thin. We decide to sit outside and watch the sky. See what it looks like now. We drag reclining lawn chairs and blankets out onto the lawn. It feels like an occasion. We are excited.

"I called the board."

Y is sitting a pot of tea on a small table between the chairs.

"I don't know why."

I lift the pot lid and stir the loose leaves.

"I work for them."

Y scoffs.

"Really? Are you sure?"

The light shifts from pink-grey to darkness just like that. Nothing gradual. No magic hour.

"They confirm anyway."

The temperature has dipped abruptly. My breath freezes the tip of my nose. Blankets.

"Ok. Good. So we go in. First thing."

Yes we do.

"They've changed the protocol for Dixon."

Y doesn't know the word.

"They want me to do it differently now."

Y exhales loud. Impatient. Hates me seeking out authority. Teen man.

"No infiltration. No finesse. They want me to find him and terminate him and whoever's in the room or on the street or near him. They think the town council has covertly requested him, that the entire town's a snake pit before he even gets there."

Y likes this. Figured he would.

"So what, we go into town and just start shooting?"

"No. That'll get us killed. We find a place to watch from. We hope we see something."

Y lays his head back and looks up.

"There's guns in the shed and the basement.

Hunting stuff. Big shotguns. A couple rifles."

I figured there was.

"We need to saw those off. Bring me the rifles in the morning. See if I can't modify them a bit. Be nice to have something automatic."

Y's arm stabs up. He points.

"Look!"

I have never seen it like this. The stars are loopy. There are fewer of them but the ones that remain are nearly as big as the moon. It's an effect of the orbit. Light bends and merges. It looks like white bulbs on a high ceiling. Polka dots, not points. At first it's breathtaking, because it's so different, then it crushes you. I feel claustrophobia. Like my breath is being pushed back into me by the sky. We are too big.

"Wow. What do you think?" Y asks.

"I think it doesn't look like it used to."

Y whistles.

"It's like you can touch it."

Y's hands wander around through the bodies of light.

A brightness low in the northern sky. Northern Lights, I think. We both watch. A long mane of prickles that spin off and fade. Then a series of puffs: pure white, silent. A few at first. Then more. The puffs appear higher. They hang, snow white then thin and drift. A couple pop closer in the sky above us.

"What is that?"

There is yellow bruising where they first appeared.

"That's people."

A sizzling red line in the bruise. It opens like a zipper and an orange column descends.

"What's happening?"

"Too many peeling at once. They're going pyroclastic."

You can see the thrust of the fires, the force. Millions of bodies cremating at once and driving all that energy into the ground. Magma from inner space punching a hole in. It is a terrifying and awesome thing to see. What if it didn't close? What if the billions came down like bath water through a drain? It would kill us all. The fires would be global. The ash would block the dying light and the heat of the sun would bounce away, never reaching us. The zipper closes. The volcano ceases. Just an ember glow. The pops continue above us. Single bodies incinerating. They look like cherry blossoms. Opening then falling apart in the wind.

"We should go inside."

"Why?"

"Well, not sure how far away that was but there's always a shockwave. Let's go in the basement."

We are in the basement for only a few minutes when it hits. Glass breaking. Furniture snapping. A heavy roar. It continues after even after the shockwave has blown past. It has left a strong wind behind.

Y has the barrel of a shotgun in a vice and he saws it. I sit with a rifle on my lap. It's semi-automatic. I am cleaning it. Oiling it. We found a man and four girls on the floor of the root cellar surrounded by broken jars of pickles and beets. They had been lying there for a long time, moving the slop around with tiny seizures. We closed it off but you can still hear them fidgeting a bit.

In the morning we climb the stairs. It is still dark. Probably the ash cloud. The floor is covered in broken glass. Window frames busted in. The door flat on its back. There's a thin dry patina over everything. Dust.

Y is sliding our guns into a bag and I stop him.

"We carry them. Lose one, you lose one. Lose the bag, you lose 'em all."

Y nods and hands me the semi-automatic and a handgun. He takes two sawed-offs and tries to hang them in belt loops. I stuff cartridges in pockets, socks, a small bag.

We eat oil and vitamin D. Drink water. Sit in the white darkness.

If the cloud clears, we'll ride. If not, we'll still ride.

rock.

There is ash drifting across Airport Road. The road dips and banks like a mad ribbon. Entire forests spring from rearing walls then fall as if dropped by a hand into bottomless valleys. It used to be beautiful. Now it looks slick with black rot. The colour is uniform. The forests are drowning in unbreathable light. The ash forms zebra marks in fallow fields. At least the cloud is thinner, higher. A light mist has turned to glue on our windshield and we have to stop to pull it back.

Y turns off this road onto a county road before we get to Avening. That's where he is.

"This where you tracked him?"

Y nods. I grant him the get. School board said he had been using the meadows behind the community hall to gather folks. I pat the scar underneath my navel. There is new muscle there. I am in old body and it has changed. I wonder if Y is. Has he been sneaking SSRIs? He seems more animated, more focused than ever. Pre-syndrome. New body. Won't last long. He appears to be much older. Deformed by this. His brow is pointed. His shoulders out-size him.

"There's an off-road lane through the woods up here. Farmers used it to access the back of fields. Let's see what we can see if we crawl in close."

Y's driving too fast. I keep forgetting he's a kid. So does he.

"Ok, pull over. I drive from here."

He stops short. Can't tell if that's just inexperience. The smell outside the car is distinct. I smell maple salmon. Clearly just that. Maple salmon. I have to stand still for a full minute before I climb into the driver's seat.

"So what's the plan? Are we going to war with a whole town?"

The maple salmon smell is in the cab now. The smell of bodies falling from the sky.

"Nope. We let them do most of the work."

The way I figure it, if the school board thinks this town is already dangerous, already lost, then I'll let Dixon strike his set before I kill him. I don't want the blood of everybody on my hands.

We see fires burning through the trees ahead. I stop the truck.

"Okay. We don't shoot anybody. Not unless they come after us."

Y nods. I'm not sure if he's relieved or disappointed. I know for a fact he is prepared to kill people. Can't tell if he's itching to.

We advance to about fifty metres of the perimeter of the field. I place Y behind a large fallen willow and I move up into the thinner trees. There are three fire pits. About four or five hundred men, women, and children gathered. They are all wearing pyjamas. Some have old-fashioned night caps on their heads. Some carry candles. There is soft singing from different groups. The sound overlaps. It is a sombre but light celebration. Kids carry stuffed toys. The flash of cameras. Strollers. A few wheelchairs.

I see no sign of Dixon, but I'm pretty sure we've crept up on the last night on earth. I fall back to the truck and wave Y over. It's three in the afternoon but it's been twilight all day. The monotonous scale of things is giving me a bit of vertigo. Lead sky, lead ground, lead light, lead morning, lead day. It was looking at my watch that made me swoon. Lead time. The trees are crudely drawn and heavily filled in. A rude hand has crushed a pencil into the heart of everything out here.

"Are we just gonna let them all die?"

Y has moved from would-be mass killer to would-be saviour in a matter of minutes. He just wants to know which one so he can finally be it and it alone. I don't answer his question. It's a good one. Am I a

killer or a saviour? I know better than that.

"Do you think he's come here? Is he gonna do his thing tonight?"

The thrum of song hangs in the forest. It's hard not to feel awe.

"I think there's a good chance."

"You wanna let them die or do you wanna kill them?"

A grackle shoots through the trees and beheads itself on a branch. There are bats out. Middle of the day. They tend to hit the ground then rise a foot or two and whoomp back down. Over and over again until they die. Now I can smell the smoke from the fires. It consumes the sickening maple salmon odour.

"They sing."

Y nods. Then looks to me. Does that mean we should let them die? Are they ready?

There he is. I can hear him. I step out of the truck and hold a hand out to Y. Stay.

I move closer but still can't hear what he's saying. Just the tone. A preacher's tone. Lifting and dropping then lifting higher. I can see him now. He's in an orange t-shirt. White hair. Thin. Can't see his face from here. But that's Dixon alright. People are sitting, listening. The occasional murmur of assent. Infant crying. There is someone beside Dixon. A woman in a brown dress. She's with him. Not town.

Dixon stops talking then the woman breaks out into song. An ancient church song. Her voice is clear and loud. Strange to hear something so clean cut through the forest. Dixon is leading a steady clap. I think things are gonna start soon. I turn to the truck, Y sits in the dark cab. I can hardly see him. I wave him out.

Y brings the guns with him. I walk back to grab mine. He is ready. His eyes are cold. I feel a need to temper this.

"This is a terrible day, Y."

Y looks frustrated.

"We are going to be part of a massacre."

Y swallows. He is sweating.

"Are we doing this?"

"You'll do what I tell you to do, but remember this: we—you and me—we didn't ask for this. We do this for a bigger reason than any we may harbour."

Y is flustered by this. It feels grey.

"We are the good part here."

Y lowers his head. That's what I wanted. Lower your head, pal. This is where we need to come from. I hook my hand around the back of his neck and give him a quick shake.

"We're gonna come out the other side of this different than we are now."

Y takes a deep breath.

"So let's respect these lives that are about to end."

Y looks up. His cold eyes are wet. Don't quite need that, actually.

"Let's know that we are cruel and that God will abandon us."

I lift his gun to his chest and bang it into him.

"It's His bad world, son."

This works. He knows what this means. He's ready again. I take him to a sheltered spot just inside the tree line. We crouch. The singing has stopped. Four men are unravelling a long cable, rolling it down the centre of the field. Several woman are positioning people along the cable. People are finding their place and holding on. Some children will not give up their stuffed toys and hang on to the cable with one hand.

"We're going to let them finish."

Y doesn't move. Doesn't react.

"I don't want to run in there shooting at women and children."

Y clenches his teeth.

"Do you?"

"No, sir."

The massive crack of electricity takes me by surprise. White spittle flies up and through the line of people. No screams. Just a horrible snapping. It doesn't stop. For a full ten minutes. Then it stops. It's darker now and hard to see the bodies. You can smell them, though. Skin scorched into flannel. Bang! I can make out the woman walking up one side of the line. Bang! The muzzle flare. She's putting down survivors. I can hear them now. Moans. Bang! She shoots another five or six times and the moaning stops.

"Okay, we run in now. You take her out and I'll get the Seller. It's dark enough that we should get pretty close before they see us. Fire when I say."

I'm going to throw your brains out on the grass, Dixon.

"Now! Go!"

We launch from the trees with our weapons up. Too much noise. I don't want a firefight in the dark. Y moves apart from me and faster. I stop, lift the gun, and put Dixon in the crosshairs.

"Dixon!"

He is thinner than I remember. Same long sharp nose. Heavy brow. That's you, buddy. Your hair's white.

"That you, phuddy?"

"I'm gonna kill ya in a second, Dix. You're gonna die."

"What for?"

"How about crimes against nature, for a start."

Dixon laughs.

"I phought that's what we do? Me and you."

The woman has walked over to Dixon. Y is moving in closer.

"Look up, Dix. Here comes God!"

I pull the trigger. Nothing.
I pull the trigger.
Y has reached the woman.
They stand side by side.
Y has emptied my gun.

pewter lakes and a plane falls.

Y must have met with Dixon while I was out in the shed. They planned this. Apparently you can choose your parents.

"We're not so different, you and I."

Dixon likes themes. I hate them.

"Let me go, Dix. I'll leave you alone."

It's not like me to beg, and in another time I might have told him to do me in. But it's a bad idea to die right here, right now. The woman is pinning my wrists with plastic cuffs.

"This is Doctor Anne."

I am led into the community centre. I'm trying to figure out how not to die. I've come close before. It's a terrible feeling. How dead are the dead? Doctor Anne sits me on a wooden chair in the middle of a stage at the front of the hall. The curtains are drawn.

Dixon leans down close to my face. He looks like a bird of prey. His large eyes set deeply back under his white brow. I can't see Y. I wonder if he can even look at me.

"Remempher us?"

Dixon isn't forming sounds correctly. I stare into his mouth. The bottom lip is slack.

"Not nice to stare. I can't make phlosive sounds. Not a phig deal. My liphs. My tongue."

You have a stroke too, Dix? Or did your mouth just get sick of you?

"Anyway, I don't talk aphout it. I have accepted it."

I can hear chairs being dragged across the floor beyond the curtain.

"I have things I want to say to you. I missed you."

Y and the doctor are not here. They are out in the hall moving chairs. Gonna be a show, I guess.

"Remempher when we killed those North Korean diphlomats in Indonesia? Then that other team in China, by the phorder?"

We were trying to start two regional wars. Not us exactly. Pender Mines.

"And we sat in that hotel. Got drunk. Watched TV with a couphle whores. Waited for one of our wars to start uph?"

One did. Pretty disappointing at the time. A border skirmish between North and South Korea. Not even the fight we were fixing.

"Too many variaphals. They should have just cleared territory on their own. They had the phower to do stuff like that."

His impediment is making my stomach roll.

"Let me go, Dix. I don't wanna die. I don't wanna go."

Dixon laughs.

"These are great times to live. You're right about that. I don't kill these pheophle, man. They kill themselves. They wanna die! And when they do, I have a little going away pharty."

Dixon believes he's the last man on earth. I can see it in his eyes. He's desperate to tell someone— me—what he's discovered.

"I have put a man's severed phenis in my rectum and you know what it did?"

I smell fried skin again.

"It swam uph my intestines like a fuckin' fish. I could see it moving uph."

I have seen what you do, Dix. I close my eyes.

"Don't close your fuckin' eyes, man!"

I feel his sharp fingertips push into my shoulders.

"I make wonders! I am dream! I am everything arriving and leaving at once!"

I let my head flop back. I don't care. I just don't want to die.

"I have a question. Do you think a dick is alive? Is it a snake? A worm? No. Dicks are much phigger than life. Life is infinitesimally small. Each spheck of

ash out there. Each half molecule of dust is shaking with life. Every goddam atom."

I picture Petra and Paula mixed in with the wet charred soup.

"So I am showing the atoms a great fuckin' time."

Dixon lifts his orange t-shirt. His gut moves. Bulges and rolling skin twist and coil in continuous motion.

"I have over a dozen pheckers in there. Sometimes they poph uph into my stomach. Only a matter of time before one sliphs up into my throat."

"Don't kill me, Dix. I work for people. I don't give a fuck what you do."

Dixon drops his shirt and lifts his prickled brow.

"You do? That's what we need. We need jobs. I got a job. I work for somephody."

Dixon stands and lays his long hands across his lower stomach.

"Curtains!"

Dixon steps aside, presenting me to an audience with his open hand.

"Phresenting, the man who would not die!"

The seats are full. All of Avening is here. Young and old. All the mothers and all the fathers and all the little children. And their bones are gnashing. Their faces have slipped. Their heads bob on strings. A man, whose naked body is entirely blackened, falls forward in the front row. A lump on his side breaks off. Y runs forward and props him back up. He places the shapeless mass, a baby, on his lap.

A banner across the back wall: "WASTECORP—Things are looking up!"

I can hear clanging sounds to my right. Metal in pans. A beep counting.

"That's right, man! Old Dix is a government dick!"

Dixon steps out centre stage and faces his audience.

"Welcome, everyone! Soon you're all going on a trip but first we have a show. Something nice to send you off with!"

Dixon turns to me. He has put lipstick on. It's blood. His lame lower lip drools.

"We get phaid pher body, phal. You folks just don't die fast enough."

"Don't kill me, Dixon. I'll do anything you want. Make me suffer. I don't give a shit. I don't want to die."

Dixon stands erect and turns on his toe.

"Folks, we have to move things along here. Phender Mines should be moving in in a few hours. We gotta get you up above the clouds!"

Someone is pulling me up. Doctor Anne. I don't resist. I don't want to be killed suddenly. Pender Mines. That's ridiculous. Dixon can say whatever he wants. Do whatever he wants. You don't need to makes sense to me, Dix. Don't even try.

"What you are aphout to witness, my friends, is a new innovation from the great minds at WasteCorph R and D. With the assistance of the lovely Doctor Anne, I intend to take you on a journey. Something for you to think about while the stars break your eyes and the sun dries your eyes."

I am guided to a gurney. Two tables are wheeled to my sides.

"Today, we change what it means to be human!"

There are silver spider nests on the tables. Complicated medical instruments. My arms are strapped in. I look up. Y is tightening. This would be the time to say something. To break through to him. To squeeze an emotion.

Y is smiling. Y is happy. Y is old.

I feel a tear leave my lower lid. Not because I have been betrayed by the boy I saved. Not because I love him. Not because I love anyone at all. Not because I am going to suffer now. Probably unimaginable torture. But because I'm pretty sure I'm going to die.

Doctor Anne wipes the crook of my arm. Clinical habit. She inserts a needle. Something to keep me alive through this. Keep me alive. I look up into Doctor Anne's face. She glances at me. Not a bad person. Not cruel. She listens to desperate pleas. I know she does. I know it.

I plead.

periodm̱$_k$m$_j$j (, GΣm$_j$G (,
GΣm$_j$G - q$_j$umlautq$_k$under.(|m̱$_j$
m̱$_k$Σq̱$_j$Σ|m$_j$

bumps in the road.

I have been unconscious. I can feel it. My hands and feet are prickling back to life. My eyes are stuck shut. I try to open them, but they won't. I believe my eyes have been sewn shut. Maybe they have crusted shut? I even out my breathing. My heart is banging through my body. I will calmly take measure of this. I will find out more.

I am alive.

I can also feel movement. A light pull in my chest. A force. Gravity behind me. There is warmth on my face. I am being moved quickly. The sun above, the earth below.

I am dead.

I try to pull my lids apart. My hands are not moving. They hang beside me, they float. My legs move in fits. Did we know this? Did we know that we don't die up here? That we feel it? That we know it? I am miles above the earth with billions of people. I need to stay calm. I need to not go mad. I breathe again. Easy, long breath. My heart begins to slow. I need to contain this. Contain myself. Take stock.

I have minimal sensation. Some of it, like breathing, might be memory, phantom breath. I have to retreat from my body. Leave my limbs. I have to change my thinking. I have to change what it means to be here. I am thought now. This relaxes me further. I am not going to die. I am not going to live. I am going to picture being here. My eyes are sealed shut. I start to think about whether this is an advantage, then I abandon the thought. I have no advantage. I have no disadvantage. When I relax, my eyes open. The light ravishes me. Sun fills my face and erases me. I feel like I am soaring. I have been distilled down to a tiny intense thrill. Soon, the whiteness separates into shapes. A circle. The moon. This light is the moon. Another circle. I feel myself bounce. I am happy. Nothing can hurt me. Nothing can stop this. I am laughing.

I am in a car. Y is driving. Dixon in the passenger seat. Ahead, a narrow hilly road. I bounce again. I turn and there is Doctor Anne's face. She says something to Dixon. I can't hear a thing. I can't feel a thing. A reflection of the road flashes across me. I am behind glass. I am in a glass case in the back seat

of a car hurtling down a country road. I'll smash the glass. I push both my fists out but they don't move. I try to kick.

My body has been wrapped. I am bound in tightly pulled linen. In a glass case. I thrash and try to roll against the glass. Doctor Anne says something again. I try to figure out if my arms are behind me or bound to my chest. I can't find them. I am much smaller. I am in a cocoon the size of log. I stop moving. They have removed my arms and legs and encased me.

I am alive.

underemployed.

There are tubes hooked up to the base of the cabinet I inhabit. Doctor Anne controls if I am asleep or wake. Among other things. I am probably fed from down there. I void through something. Into something. I have just woken again and my lids are stuck together again. My eyes are not lubricating properly. The rest of me is run from below. My eyes, however, are being maintained by no one. I stop trying to open them. Last time they opened on their own. Had I cried? Was that it? I'm not sure if I can even manage crying right now. Where would I start?

I am moving. A regular bounce. Someone is carrying me. I must be very small now. My head bobs on my neck. I'm being carried sideways. They wouldn't kill me now, would they? I'm pretty elaborate. You don't make elaborate things then destroy them. No. I am a trophy. I am turned upright. Then turned upside down. My eyes fly open. Y is holding me. Turn me right way around! Turn me! I can feel gurgling beneath me. Fluids are going in the wrong direction. A pair of hands land on the case. Doctor Anne. She turns me up.

I can only hear faintly what's going on outside. I can tell she isn't happy. I remember those days. An orange t-shirt. Dixon's hands. The pads on his fingers are crystal clear on the glass. They pull slightly as he takes my case. I can see people in the distance. Picnic tables. Trees. A band shell. Not Avening. Where are we? Dixon puts me down. I can see him frantically explaining something to Doctor Anne.

Y has moved up onto the band shell and is setting up some kind of display. There is a long banner. WASTECORP ANNUAL PICNIC. I sense something close. The faces of two children close to the glass. A girl points, her finger presses. Dixon knocks her hand down. She looks up, big eyes and heavy lips. What am I supposed to be?

I am lifted again and swept up onto the stage. I am sat on the display table. I watch Dixon step out centre stage. His arms rise and fall as he talks. He is very animated. A trophy? Maybe I'm an oracle. A holy relic. I can see the audience looking past Dixon to me. I lay the back of my head on the glass. My neck is sore. My neck reacts as if the rest of my body was active. The vestigial ghost of me. I wonder how far my spine goes down or if I'm sitting on a soft tube of organs. I can clench my stomach. She must have seen the scar there. Y might have told her how he saved my life in an abandoned car behind the Home Hardware. From a distance I can see how they both must take pride in me. I am something wonderful they share. I am what they did.

I hear Dixon's voice.

"And phehold! The future of life on earth is Syndrome! It takes us all! And it takes us phiece by phiece! The nerves of the back are ground to pulph by its own great column! The feet are withered and droph off! The victim of morning-onset diaphetes! A million sclerotic nerves biting the toes off like children's teeth crack candy! The calves give in to desphair and phointlessness, phecoming fetid lunch for maggots! While cancer of the phone casts off all ligaments and muscle as the marrow drains clean as a straw dropping milk! The shoulders fall like phad apples! The arms! The hands! Who knows what sly new infirmity snatched them off! The kiln-fired liver! The immophile heart! Dead colon and sphleen! What can this worm in time ask for? What will we want? We can only ask!"

The audience is all open mouths and silent. Children perched on shoulders. Dixon walks back to me and leans down. He unlatches the door to the case. He puts his ear to my mouth. I will tell them the truth. I go to speak but can only mumble. I have no tongue. They cut out my tongue. I cannot tell them anything. Dixon rises and covers his face. He staggers to the front of the stage. He speaks in a hushed intimate voice full of candour and gravity.

"It has sphoken to me. Do you want to know what it said?"

Heads nod.

"Do you?"

Several shout.

"Do you want to know what your future is saying to you?"

More shouts. Dixon raises a hand and the audience stops. Some of the children are brought down off shoulders and held.

"It wants to be free."

Silence.

"It wants to be free!"

The audience erupts. It isn't a cheer, really, more a chorus of shouts—anger and agreement and some dissent and keening. Dixon rushes back to me and violently swings my case in the air.

"It is crying for you! Phehold the tears!"

I am crying. Not for them. Though if there was more to me I might. I cry because I have just discovered that my tongue has been cut from my mouth.

The audience is now spellbound. This got them. I

look upward to heaven. I don't know what I want. I want to be Holy. I want belief from them. I am not human.

Dixon drops me back into place. I see Y reach the centre of the stage. I am sad when he speaks. I remember when he couldn't.

"Forms are down here to my left. We do have orbit charts and placements for a placement fee. Please line up!"

The door to the case is closed and latched and I am returned to my muffled world. The smell of linen and liniment. The pumps and engines beneath and their hums and puffs. A black cloth is pulled over my case. In the darkness I can see a red dot blink, reflected in the glass.

The next several days are spent like this. I am moved from time to time, but mostly I sit in darkness listening to the little machines attached below. I learn the new smell of my feces, feces which I will never see again. It smells like pencil shavings. Pencil shavings and vinegar. Occasionally I open my mouth and howl. It's an upsetting sound. A walrus bark. I learn that I do have muscle. Across my back to the two points at the base of my neck. And down to the edges. I use them just to feel them. I tell myself I am going for walks and I flex them. I wish they hadn't taken my tongue. That is the worst thing. I can no longer say if I am awake or dreaming and have decided they are one and the same.

The audience. The preacher. The forms. The hood is pulled off and the event repeated. I do not cry anymore so now the doctor puts drops in my eyes before I am revealed. Each time it is less crisp, less real. I find myself sailing over their heads, wanting only to be returned to my case and my silence and my darkness.

everyone i see is dead now.

I am planning to escape. It will not be easy. I am a limbless, mute baby in a sealed vault. I can rock. I have been trying this, mostly as a comfort, but my back and stomach muscles are getting stronger. I could wait until I am hoisted up above their heads, with the door thrown open and then I could rock and tip forward and fall. Then what? Fall into someone's arms. I cannot chose that person or what they will do. I cannot tell them what I want them to do. I can pray. I can pray that I land in the arms of a teen mom who lost her rape baby. She would hold me fast and flee. Take me away from town. To a river winding in a shallow valley. I would suck her breasts. I pray that the milk would make me grow. I would grow arms and legs. I have trouble picturing them though. A nightmare always intrudes. The arms and legs are small bones hanging lose like plastic on a dime store Halloween doll. My tongue inflates and crushes me. An immense scarred manatee attached to the roof of my mouth. No. It's impossible. If I managed to fall out of this case the crowd would jump back and I'd land in the dirt. My little machines smashed. I would die. I cannot die.

Some of the towns I don't recognize. We are moving south-eastward I think. I recognize Beeton. Beeton is mad. They press against the stage with their arms straight up. They're in holy ecstasy. That's when I realized I truly am a divine relic. I am a piece of cross. A Saint's tibia. You see? You see us now, Oh Lord? I am pure. No hands to reach out and strike or steal or grope. No legs to run on, to escape justice, to stomp out with. No penis to cram into faces and mouths. No tongue to lie with. I am a singular message. I am here. That is all, Lord. I am here.

Beeton is frightening. These people were waiting for us. Fathers and mothers stepping on their children just to touch the glass of my case. Sick old women draped across the front of the stage like fish dying on a riverbank. We are in the centre of Main Street here. Not in some parking lot, or remote park tucked away. We are now a popular travelling roadshow. Stacks of flyers in shoulder bags. Traffic cops swinging their arms. I spot the mayor on the sidewalk. He has his heavy red sash on. He looks terrified. Aware and sane. There are some, frantic moms pulling their children back. The majority, however, reach for me across the stage. Four teenage girls rush the stage and throw babies over heads. The babies, likely rape babies, are wrapped in bloody blankets. One tumbles out. No arms or legs. No limbs because the limbs have been cut off. They are dead. The teen moms flee amid cheers. Dixon shakes his fists above the fray, pleading and crying to the grey sky. I notice Y on a chair at the edge of the stage. He has a bandage wrapped around his thigh. He must have tried to cut his leg off.

People want to be me.

Later that night we begin the mass launch. This time the cable is thrown down the middle of main street. I watch as the cable is pulled taut down two blocks of maple-lined street. Police hold people back on the sidewalks while connections are made and tested.

I hear the anabolic shriek of table saws and clattering glottis of chainsaws. Stations are set up in storefronts for people who wish to be dismembered before they go. The first few are the most zealous and they endure the blades with eyes cast upward in frozen joy. Freshly removed arms and legs are passed across a sea of risen hands. Genitals are flung up into trees and telephone wires. The reduced torsos rolled to the cable where they bleed out in seconds. Soon blood has caught everyone. Shirtless men and women pat themselves with sticky red palms. Faces plastered with rich dark hair. Bright ghost shapes on windows. The next wave of dismemberment is not as deliberate. This wave is changing its mind having seen the first. This wave has to be pushed to the saws, held down by many hands. Some wiggle free, made slippery by their own blood. They spring howling though the crowd. Some have one arm and a shoulder spraying mist across the crowd. Some have only deep cuts and they bounce from brick walls like animated scarecrows. Order dies. The crowd no longer looks to the stage. There are too many screaming machines. Too much blood and running corpses. Whirling blenders that make their way into the crowd. They are seeking their own completion now. Dixon turns back to me. He gestures to Y. Time to go. Throw the damn switch and let's move on.

The cable explodes down the middle of the street and hundreds of people seize up at once. Others leap on and are crunched into balls by the voltage. Blood pools blacken and are lit with fury. Several heavy men move in, driving chainsaws through backs and necks until the current finds them and they become still, still like memorial statues. Dixon lifts me and I am placed in the truck. The crowd that is still able to move moves on us. I watch the faces of people throwing themselves onto the windows. These are not the faithful anymore. These ones have been shattered, they have awoken angry and afraid.

They are yelling at me. Pounding the window. We are running away form what we started. They know it.

Y shoots those hanging off the drivers' side. Several bullets pierce glass and slip into upholstery. Dixon uses a hammer to cave in the skulls of people in his way. The truck starts and pulls forward, but the hands of the frenzy hold us back. The tires spin and burn in place. Dixon turns to me and signals the doctor to hold my case. He throws it in reverse and the wheels bounce across bodies. When he throws it into drive, we fishtail on the guts and muscle and bone. The tires burn through the skin and grab the road. We shoot forward and plough through those ahead. I hear Dixon call out like a cowboy. We are under the heavy sopping skirts of flesh blood. Torn arms and butterflied faces. The contents of stomachs, the undersides of lost heads. Dixon reverses again, this time opening a patch of sky. There is a live cable on the ground somewhere. The rubber tires protects us but the blood could conduct it. We break through the body knots and are free. Dixon guns it and we hit a light standard. The truck turns and the standard falls, pulling people down and folding them. I see flames. The crowd has ignited and the living are like freshly lit matches, their hair bright orange and yellow. The truck is heading out from the centre of town. I can no longer see what is happening behind us.

I used to have the ability to be moved by things

like this. Horrified. I wonder if my emotion might have been in my arms all along, my legs, my testicles. Gone. All I care about is getting away in time. When you can't move on your own anymore there is no such thing as a place to stay.

The windshield wipers are stirring up a pink foam. We have to pull over. We are east of Beeton on the 8th Line. Y is taking water in a pail from the ditch and throwing it onto the car. Dixon has walked down the road. The doctor sits beside me, her head turned. I want to look back. Is the town a fireball? Are they running up the road with their heads lit up? Y gets back in the driver's seat and sits. Dixon returns. He reaches back and flips open the front of my case.

"Can we get him out of there easy?"

The doctor reaches in and plays with the hook-up below. She nods.

"Yes. Why?"

Dixon rubs his lips hard. They must be numb. He has no feeling in his mouth. That's the impediment.

"We're going to change some things. No more phosters. Too much hype. I don't want things haphening we can't control. Who phrought the saws? Is that on any of the phosters? How did all this shit haphen?"

Y sighs. The doctor fiddles with my bottom.

"The new rule is we keep things calm. I got an idea."

Dixon looks into my face. A look of surprise.

"Ha! How's it going, phal? I almost forgot that was you in there. Listen uph. I want to try something. Next time, we phring the Oracle out and we phass it around."

Y's head is deep in his hands, elbows on the lower scoop of the wheel. There are white strands of hair bending up from the crown. He is several ages as far I can tell.

"It'll calm them. Give them something to be careful with. I want an orderly burn. We made no fucking money in Pheeton and we might even get phulled in."

Y starts the truck. Y knows why Beeton failed.

"Beeton was crazy before they met us. Pond Head'll be better. Smaller. More churches."

Dixon slaps Y on the shoulder.

"That's right, son. Phond Head. But not too soon. Let's phe missed for a while. Let 'em wonder if we're real for a while."

We don't turn south to Bond Head. We head up towards the 9th. We're looking for trees or a house. I'm surprised to see cars on the road. Not many, but some. They look normal, timeless. Some lone drivers. Male mostly. One car full of a family. I try to read faces but they blow past too quickly. Cars and trucks at farmhouses. Cattle. It's as if nothing happened. Could be the way this part of the country lives. Nothing is supposed to happen here. You can see too far. A small fishing boat for sale. The trailer tires flat. The posted price on swollen cardboard. If terrible things were approaching they would be seen hours before they arrived.

The truck slows and we pull up a dirt driveway. We lurch along its length and stop under a willow beside a massive red brick farmhouse. We sit in silence. The house is still. Thin pale leaves drift down and attach to blood clots under the wipers. Dixon shoves Y's shoulder. Y shoots a look then opens the door. He walks cautiously around the front of the house. Dixon rolls his window down.

"Go knock."

Y is tense. He takes the steps, counting.

"Knock!"

Y knocks and waits. Again.

"Ophen the door! Yell for 'em."

Y doesn't look back. He slowly draws the screen open, then the inner door. We hear his voice but not what he is saying. Y steps back out and waves. Clear.

"Okay. Well. This is a nice place."

Dixon isn't getting out just yet.

"Maybe we should retire here."

A Rottweiler, moving like a barrel down a sluice, bursts through a hole in the backyard fence. It doesn't bark until it sees Y, then it makes a killing noise. Y stops in mid-step.

"You gotta kill that!"

"Help!"

Y runs for the truck. The door locks, clunk.

"Kill the damn dog!"

"What?"

Y reaches the car with the dog. It springs up and grabs Y by the jaw, dragging him down.

Dixon roots through the glove box and finds a road flare. He opens the driver's window and drops it.

"Shove this down its throat!"

Dixon rolls the window back up and waits. We hear the intense hiss of the flare igniting and then the dog cry out. Dixon waits, then rolls down the window.

"You there?"

The dog appears around the front of the truck. It doesn't appear to be wounded but it ain't a killer no more either. Not for now. It slinks back through the torn fence.

Dixon opens the door.

"Okay. Okay. Good job. I'm sorry. We got a doctor."

The farmhouse smells of cows. The floors curve and the walls bow. Discoloured shapes on the ceiling form a map of the world. If you stare long enough you can see places you want to go. The doctor takes Y upstairs. He's going to be okay. Some punctures on his scalp. A burn up his arm from the flare.

Dixon sets me up on the table as he goes through

a pail he found inside the front door.

"This is the house of Phauline Hartenpherger. Lived alone. Oh. Wait. No. One kid at least. Goes to, went to, Byng Elementary school. This interest you at all?"

I say nothing. I pretend not to notice. I am still a prisoner.

Dixon opens, reads, and drops papers to the floor.

"Child support. Good for you, Pheter Hartenpherger. I got married, you know."

Dixon is sharing. He's proud.

"Yes, sir. After Indonesia. Her name was Phie. Like a phizza. We lived in Meaford. I had a daughter, too. Her name was Lo."

Dixon is reading a phone bill. I wonder if you can see changes in a phone bill. Patterns. Times. Frequency of calls to the same number. Did the Hartenbergers make plans, then leave? Did they flee to the city? Did they hang themselves? Maybe they're out back. Cold black bones on the clothesline.

"You wanna know what haphened to them? Got caught in the first raphe wave. Died."

Dixon drops the phone bill. He straightens the pages and returns them to the envelope.

"I dropphed 'em in a well."

Dixon reads signs on the wall. Happy Home. Live. Love. Laugh.

"You know what I love to do? Hmmm? I love

a pheaceful launch. I like to sphend time with them phefore they go. Get a little carried away, sure, phut . . ."

Dixon thinks he's different now. He wants to have a different past. If I was to mention that he has worn dead children he would think me vulgar. You don't know anything, he'd say. Dixon wants to believe that he held out as long as he could. That if he's a hero he's only doing what anyone would do. And if he's evil, it's only the role he is forced to play. I expect him to cry. The doctor comes in and goes to the sink.

"Hi."

Dixon is being ridiculous in this setting. The doctor turns, surprised.

"There's beds upstairs. Lots of food in the cellar. Preserves. Tins. Some household medicines. Some antibiotics."

"What's Y doin'?"

"He's checking the barn. We can kill a cow. How long are we here?"

Dixon pushes the remaining letters to the floor. He opens the fridge and gas erupts from rotting food. He gags and closes the door.

"I dunno. WasteCorph is gonna be looking for me to check in. They're gonna have lots to say aphout Pheeton."

The doctor has been washing her hands for ten minutes.

"Beeton was fine."

She swipes a cloth from the oven door and pats dry her hands.

"I have no problem with Beeton."

Dixon slumps a bit. She has cheated him. The doctor stares at me for a long minute. She takes in a sharp breath and looks at Dixon.

"I would like to have sex. Can you?"

Dixon laughs with his loose face.

"Nophe."

The doctor is disgusted.

"Oh, that's right. You only fuck parts of people."

Dixon stretches his neck as if that will change how he appears to her.

"Go fuck the phoy. He can. I think."

The doctor drops the cloth into a silver trash can.

"I will. Thank you."

bounty.

The dog proves to be a nuisance. It circles the house in the tall grass waiting for us to come out. It grabbed Y again and he managed to gouge out an eye before it rolled off him. Dixon doesn't seem overly worried. I think it's a game he likes. He likes to send Y out. The doctor spends a lot of time upstairs alone. She showers several times a day. They eat beets and jam and beans. For a while the doctor tried to breast feed me but no milk came. I eat bean juice. There is lots of time to think here. The days are slow. If a car goes by on the road it's a major event. We hide and shout and sit in the dark. Dixon is thinking more than anyone. He sits and stares at things. Or he finds things in the house to read. He reads grocery lists. Recipes. He hunts for journals and diaries but finds none. He sits with a receipt in his hand and thinks. He rubs and curls the receipt until it's a ball in the palm of his hand, then he drops it. I know what he's doing. He wants to show the relic that he cares about these people's lives. I know he doesn't. I know he would do obscene things to them after they were destroyed. He has been looking at me differently. This slow world is revolving us. Y comes in with the dog. It is draped across his shoulders. Headless.

"Would we eat dog?"

Dixon pushes back his chair and rises.

"Phut it on the phicnic table. We'll clean it there."

Y stands for a moment.

"Don't I get a hurray or something?"

Dixon seems drunk.

"Oh. Yeah. Sure."

Y holds the base of the tail at his shoulder and wags it.

"I slew the beast!"

Y looks to me. I am not that type of person anymore. You don't look me in the eyes. Methusela Syndrome. That's what you got. Accelerated aging.

"Okay. I'll get some knives."

I can only see the tops of their heads gathered around the picnic table. They are skinning it. Gutting it. Seems to me I've seen cows in fields around here. Surely we could snatch one at night. Y holds the dog's head up. Gore slaps his forehead.

They're doing this because it keeps them in touch with the mission. The doctor has taken to roaming the house topless. It arouses me but I have no penis. Some veins throb in my anus. That's my limit. She is washing her hands at the sink. Her back is broad and white. It's a cooling sight. They are hammering Rottweiler hide to a sheet of plywood. They want to dry it in the sun. The sun is a joke. Nothing dries in the sun. Maybe the wind. The cold, wet wind. The doctor pulls the window pane to the side. She tries to close it in a single swipe but it jams and she gives up.

"I'm not eating a fucking dog."

The doctor dries her hands, points at me then leaves, climbing the stairs to her room.

Dixon and Y spend the afternoon outside butchering the dog and digging a fire pit. Y finds an iron pole to skewer it. I can see they are laughing. They toss guts and skin and legs and head into a barrel, then sticks. They pour gasoline in. It flares out in a massive ghost ball then dies out. They give up.

The doctor runs down the stairs and out the door. Something's up. I wish they wouldn't close my case. I wish they'd let me in. I can see Dixon's serious face as he listens to the doctor. Y is bent down, probably turning the dog.

Dixon comes in first and goes up the stairs. The

doctor follows him. Y tries to come in but Dixon sends him back.

"You stay outside."

Y takes a step back but stays. Listening.

There is a small piece of glass missing now at the top of my case. In the right conditions I can make out what people say.

In time Dixon comes down. He walks in heavy steps. He is perspiring. He speaks close to the doctor and I can't hear. She listens, then bends back to spot Y.

"Well, Dixon. It's okay. We do our work."

Dixon nods severely. He raps the wall once and comes over to me. He pulls the black bag over my case. I am a thin black wisp of hair. I am black crayon on a black sky. My knees buckle and I go down.

I sleep because I haven't slept. I sleep in a closed-off dreamless airless box.

A band of light wakes me. Someone has cut an almond-shaped hole in the bag. Someone cuts another hole. These are eyeholes. They want me to see. I feel a rush of hopefulness. They are including my care. I am to be given light. Not to keep me alive. But to bring me comfort. The thought makes me dizzy. I feel my knees again. I look out one of the eye holes. The doctor's shoulder. I can see her and she cannot see me. A vein in my anus fills and rolls on its side. The light makes a perfect cone over my eye. We are going upstairs. We are going upstairs. The topless doctor is taking me to her room. The case is tipped against the wall while she opens the door. I see the top of her breast rise under her turning arm. It's an achingly soft surface. The breast drops from view as the door opens. She points me forward to a curtained window. Drops me on the sill and turns me. There is a wide unmade bed. The doctor removes her skirt. She rolls her pantyhose down, then drops them from her toes. She walks toward me. Her large black-grey bush is inches from my nose. I can see the lips of her vagina. The slow separation of tissues relaxing. She is hanging her hose on the rail above me. She can't see me while I cling to the details of her hole. My lower half is bunched. Veins an open confusion. I can feel my cock springing to life on a wall. On the ground. She turns and walks to the bed, bending over to pick up her clothes. Light touches her asshole for a second then she stands again. My bottom shatters. I am filling something with something. A spasm. I feel warmth. I must be shitting. I push at it hard. I want to feel it come out. I want to feel my body express itself. I want it out.

She is gone. I stop holding my breath. I smell gas. I haven't shit. I have farted. A wonderful changing and calming fart.

there is no upside.

I sit in this box for hours. Maybe longer. I hear a car door close outside and a man's voice. People down below. Must be WasteCorp. They want an account of Beeton. Probably needed to bring in a clean-up crew. I've been on them. Different company, different war. The doctor came in once and took something she'd stashed inside her pillow. I see you, Doctor. I know you're in trouble. SSRIs in the pillowcase. I decide that because I am non-human, a deity of some kind, that I should be able to close my eyes and see great things, visit exotic places. Even if this isn't true, shouldn't the mind provide? Can't I just go completely mad and leave this? Go so far inward that I'm a new thing? I close my eyes and wait. I try to picture simple things. A shoe. A bottle. A tree. I can only manage fleeting lines and shadows.

The door opens. The doctor enters. She is fully clothed. Her bosses are here. She comes over to me and turns the box. I see the yard clearly through my hole. There are two black vans parked up the driveway. So that's WasteCorp, I guess. Guys dressed like milkmen from another century. Smart blue capos and white piping on the legs. Not tough guys, that's for sure. Dixon and Y are up by one of the old maples. A bald man in a black suit is showing Dix something on a wide unfolded sheet. Plans have been drawn up. Things are being done differently. Beeton shook them up, bad. The milkmen unroll a wide mesh mat. It reaches all the way to Dix and the tree. Size of a football field. Milkmen attach cables at each corner. No more coaxing folks to toe the line. No more people running off or letting go too soon. They're going to sit them down for the show, then just burn 'em all where they sit. Y and Dixon are walking the perimeter. I can tell by the way Dixon walks, with a repressed swagger, that he doesn't like something. He doesn't like seeing his bosses. Doesn't like them being here. Don't fuckin' tell me how to do my job. Dixon and Y have walked up into the house. The milkmen straighten out any creases in the mat, like old women showing off patchwork at the fall fair.

The doctor turns me around. I see her naked

thigh through the hole. I feel my anus drop then pull in. She drags the black bag up. Her tits are fat against the glass. She opens the door. Her breasts smell like change room. I look up and she looks down. I am brought out to the bed. She lies me near the bottom then drops her legs on either side of me. I watch as she pushes against her vagina with three fingers. She pumps it then slides her fingers back and forth quickly. With her other hand she tugs her nipple, lifting her large breast then letting it fall. It is a mesmerizing and mechanical sequence of actions. No hurry. I am to watch this. She wanted an audience. She wants me to stare at her pussy. Her heavy tits. She slides a finger in deeply. A clear fluid runs down her wrist. She makes a sound. She draws her knees up slowly and reaches under. Now she has a finger in her asshole and three in her pussy. She works the two holes at different speeds. The vagina is occasionally pulled and the finger in her anus drops out and turns briefly on her sphincter. She looks up from time to time to see if I'm watching. No smile, nothing, just a check. I feel a buzzing near my bottom. Peripheral neuropathy. My anus feels as if hard beads are vibrating in it. She points a wet finger at me and curls it. She wants me there. I rock slowly, moving on my corners.

Her pussy meets my face and I feel her hands on the back of my head. I cannot breathe. She holds my head tight against her. I feel my lung climbing into my throat. My lung is my tongue. I panic and shake my face. Her thighs start to close, then she shoves me back hard. I breathe quickly. I can smell her pussy. Rainwater and salt. Below that, the heavy sugar of her asshole. She pulls me in again. This time I suck. I take her entire vagina into my mouth and suck. I can breathe through one nostril. She pulls me in tighter to seal it. I lose consciousness for a brief second. When I come up, I'm gasping. I hear my buttonhole whistle and she shakes. The doctor reaches down on my body and lifts my back end. She lays me on her belly so my face hangs down over her lips. I flick. The sensation of her tongue on my anus makes me jump. She twirls around slipping the tip in and out. I feel that if this is to proceed much longer I may die. I don't have the body to withstand this. Maybe that's what she wants. She wants to kill me with her tongue up my ass. Before I reach whatever it is that could happen, she pushes me down. My tongue slips from her pussy to her anus and I try to breath normally as I do to her what she did to me.

There is someone else in the room. I feel the bed dip. I try to raise my head to see but can't. The bedsprings twang under the weight of three. I feel the doctor's finger in my ass. Deeper. Bigger. It's not a finger. Its a cock. Someone is sitting on her face and sliding his cock into my flat, featureless body.

I hear her slurping and suck his ass and balls. Her pussy rises under my chin. I am supposed to suck, too. I draw her clit in while she flips fingers inside. The cock is now fully in me and has begun to pump. The tissue in my hole is banging and open. The doctor starts to come first. She clamps my cheeks with her thighs and starts to buck. The cock in me reaches deeper and faster. I feel the fat tip punching through me into the mattress. A series of sensations run up and down my entire body, like hoops across a levitated showgirl. The hoops multiply and crash, meeting in my back then plunging dramatically into my anus. I can't tell who is moving now. No one maybe. The air is glittery and colour is thick. Her legs fall. The cock dives forward once then slips back and out. I turn my head so my ear shell is on her pudenda. I see a tee shirt on a chair. Brown not orange.

as you were.

I am back in my box and under my hood. I am faced out to see this evening's show. The vans are gone. We're on our own. Dixon will like this. After we finished on the bed no one spoke a word. The doctor said nothing as she dressed. Y shot me a look before he left. A wet filthy grin. He's a dirty old man now. The doctor placed me here. I see her now below, leading families to spots on the mat. Y is lying in the grass under a tree. Dixon is greeting on the driveway. I remember when we first heard about the dead not dying. We were told they were predators, killers, cannibals. Now we are making the dead. The window is closed and so is my case so I won't hear what's being said. I have a great view though. The mat now nearly full. The line of trees back to the road. And beyond that a wide hill specked with cattle.

The mat is lit with no warning. This is the new way. They are not brought to it by an evangelist. There is no ecstatic moment, no praise, no Oracle. The mat contains a powerful jolt. It lights up like an overly full bug zapper. People shake and pop and sizzle. It lasts no more that a minute. In the darkness I see clothes and bodies glowing, then they fade. The scene remains like this for some time. Black fog rising. Silence. Headlights on the road. WasteCorp is leaving. Dixon is a janitor now.

The door opens behind me. I sense two people on either side of me. Doctor and Y. They look out.

"He's not happy."

"They told him to go inside. To watch."

"What do you think he's going to do? "

They step back from the window. The doctor turns on a night table lamp. She removes her clothes, draping them over a chair. I close my eyes. I'm not ready to do that again. The ceiling light goes out. I open my eyes. The doctor gets into her side of the bed and leans on her elbow. She draws a paper out and starts to read. Y is turned away in the dark. The front door bangs. Dixon. I try to see into the dark yard but he has turned the porch light off. I hear his chainsaw start up. I decide to watch the doctor's reflection as she reads. Her black hair is bunched up by the pillow and looks bouffant. There is a tail of grey across her shoulder. She turns the page. The chainsaw screams in the oil slicks just beneath her reflection. I lean my head back to rest against the case. I fall asleep.

I am woken by the sound of bed wheezing. They are fucking. I lean up to the eyehole just to confirm then drop back.

I am woken by yelling downstairs. I check the eyehole but they are still in bed. The doctor is reading again. Dixon is breaking the place downstairs and bellowing like a moose. The doctor's light goes out.

I have been moved while I slept. I am at the top of the stairs looking down. The stairs are worn and shiny. People are in the kitchen but I can't hear what they say. The voices sound calm. I guess they are getting ready to leave. I wonder about being left behind. There's a grandfather clock on the wall at the base of the stairs. Stopped at 4:35. I must look a bit like his son. Framed pictures on the walls going down. I can't see them at this angle. Not hard to guess what they look like. The mom. The kid on a pony. The dog.

The doctor backs in from the kitchen. I strain, listening.

"No. I think this is good news. Give me a second."

She turns and briskly makes the climb, sidestepping around me.

I want her to be careful coming back. I don't want her to accidentally knock me down the stairs.

Y swings around the corner, one hand hooks the door frame. He's up, two steps at a time. I am lifted, quickly, like last luggage in the hall and descend sideways under Y's arm.

In the kitchen I face the stove. The oven window has been smashed. The range hood is crumpled and pulled down like a prom dress.

"How are we supposed to carry that big mat thing?"

"They left us a trailer. I did it all last night."

I bet you did, Dix.

"Where is she?"

"I'll go get her."

Y hands my case to Dixon. I see him stare blankly. He's not going to take it.

"Phut him outside."

I am here again. I am on a stage again. Dixon is there again swinging his arms like a bat man. The crowd is there again, their stupid faces deformed by fat bones. Saliva and pustules and missing teeth and fingers and arms. This is a late crowd. I am the One. I am the Oracle. I am a dead Disney princess.

I see something. Something no one else can see.

In the sky far behind the crowd and the buildings, slowly descending funnel of night and fire. The great ring is falling at seven hundred kilometres an hour, a thousand degrees Centigrade. The great pink death is about to fall on us. I hear the boom, then seconds later the glass bangs and a crack appears. Dixon stumbles back. The crowd drops to the ground. Y runs around in front of me, his balance is thrown. I can't see the doctor. She may be gone. The rumbling earth beneath my case. This is the death we need. This is a good death.

Dixon runs to the display, to me. I am his most important possession. We've come a long way, Dix. Let's go out with a bang. Just before the hood comes down I see Dixon's eyes catch fire. His teeth fly from his gums. A far away whip has been cracked and its hot tip flips the brain from the preacher's skull.

A blast punches my case and I leave the ground. Hot air has filled the hood and sent me into the air. I don't know how high I am. If I'm ahead or above or inside. The case flies end over end like a manic hourglass in an epileptic's fist. A panel has shattered and the glass snips my face. I want to go up. I want to go. The air is like a beast. It roars and strikes and twists. It stops. Silence. Wind.

Light is leeching up from the base of me. Cold fresh air is filling the sac. I am floating.

I land in water and it rushes in to drown me. I am tired of dying. I am tired of sleeping. Soon I will be tired of breathing.

It just so happens that I am pulled from the stream by a senile old woman who thinks I am a baby, probably Moses, and takes me back to her house on a hill so she can raise me to deliver her people from bondage.

Apple purée is amazing. I could live on that. Not liquid rice. That is dreadful stuff. Makes me squirt. Tildy has gone to the city today. She explained that it could be dangerous for babies so she has left me in the care of her dog. Candy is a miniature dachshund. She bites. I am only slightly larger than her but our shapes are remarkably similar. On Candy's birthday, Tildy painted my white wrap black and tan and she darkened my nose. She laid me down beside the dog and clapped. Candy tore the shell of my ear before Tildy could get me back up. Today I am in a high chair far enough away from Candy's barracuda moods. The tray before me is a flowerbox of straws and baby food.

I have a nice view of the wide valley through the bay window. It is white from the cooled pyroclastic flow. Tildy's house is high enough up the rim that it was spared. The sky is still black. Been like that for weeks. Tildy has an oil furnace and she keeps the house warm. She tells me that it is like January out there. It's July. The baby food and formula is giving me astonishing nutrients. I'm pretty sure we will die

soon. The oil will run out. The food. Some hungry man will eat us. For now, though, this is the most at peace I have ever been in my life. In the morning Tildy gives me tummy time on her bed and I roil from side to side. Her comforter is thick and deep and smells like tea. In the afternoon she sits in the corner and reads from the Bible by candlelight. There is no sun and the only ambient light comes up from the white shell of cold ash in the valley. It gives off a surprising shine.

Tildy thought for while that I was the baby Moses. She said she ran down the hill that awful day, toward the fire. She says she wanted it. The rapture. She didn't want to be left behind. And when she ran through the stream she saw the torn black hood. My face inside. Eyes closed and body swaddled. She claims there were bulrushes but I'm pretty certain she made that up. In time she forgot this thread, me being the baby Moses. The day-to-day work of looking after a baby was enough for her tired old mind. There seems to be little Syndrome in her. Her dementia is light and honest. The elderly don't manage neurotransmitters. They believe it is correct to die one day. There is a sadness to Tildy too. She must have had children and grandchildren. A husband. They are probably gone now. Delivered to the sun or burnt by those who fell from the sun. She hums.

Candy is sitting on the settee. Her head is on a pillow and her eyes rock warily from side to side. Occasionally she growls at me. I like her company as long as I am safe. The little machines broke away from my bottom. I must have a stomach after all. You lied about that Dixon. I also have not had a return of Syndrome. And I sleep. In a bassinet beside my Tildy. I constipate easily and I upchuck two or three times a day. Candy gives out a short bark. She springs up on her tiny legs. Someone is here. I see Tildy in her yellow parka dragging heavy cloth bags. She found some things in the city. Candy barks and whines at the door. I try to tell her to stop but only manage sounding like her, only weaker.

The door opens and I feel the cold curl into the room. Snow or dust or ash drifts inside.

Tildy heaves the bags up on the table and slides her fur-lined hood back. She puffs her red cheeks then smiles. She pulls a sac of dog treats out and drops them for Candy while making dove sounds.

"Well, Moses."

She still calls me that though it's not meaningful anymore.

"I didn't get to the city, little man, but I did manage to find a warehouse outside of Mansfield. Not a store proper. Some kind of warehouse and I borrowed some things!"

Tildy lines up the jars of baby food. A tall can of

dry formula. Some bags of frozen milk. A stack of three or four TV dinners. She'll make a fire in the woodstove and heat those. I smile and clap my imaginary hands.

"There's nobody out there, Mosey. Not a soul. Seems like end of days more than ever. Oh, well. Never mind. We got each other and a warehouse down the road."

Tildy laughs at her wickedness. I watch her scooping dry formula into a bottle and fill it with water. She repeats this several times then sets all but one just outside the door to freeze. The dead are frozen now. I wonder if they still move. Those seizures and tiny fits cracking the ice in their bones. Maybe shattering them over time. Shards of lung and crystallized eyes. Tildy shakes the bottle I am to drink. She won't give it to me yet though. She wants to warm it. She sits on it.

The Bible. I listen, mostly to her voice. Her quiet amens. I don't care what the words mean as much as I love Tildy's calm, happy voice. She stops from time to time, closing the book on her speckled fingers and she looks out to the dead world as if it were a field of bright yellow wheat. As if her children were running through the grass up the hill. Or angels. She drifts off. We have all the time we need, Tildy and I.

I am genuinely grateful to be here. I have been a violent man. I have brought many people to sudden death. Now I am bundled and free of limbs and speech and pain. I squeeze a small turd through my buttonhole. I watch Tildy sleep. Candy. The black sky and the silver earth. These days can end or not end. I am home.

Tildy wakes when the room temperature falls. It is cold in here. I can see cloud puff from my mouth.

"That's bitter in here, Mosey. I'll check the furnace."

Tildy returns after almost an hour. The house is now becoming dangerous. She doesn't look at me or say anything as she pulls on her parka. She stomps a boot to keep Candy from the door and she leaves.

Candy walks in a military march toward me then stops and takes her post. She knows as much as I do. She is visibly shivering.

We sit like this, staring each other down for about a half hour, when the door opens. Nine or ten frozen logs fall in with a shroud of dry white particles. I only see Tildy's arm as she pulls the door closed again. Candy barks and runs to the settee. The cold floor hurts her paws.

Tildy does this three more times until the entire front room is dominated by logs. I can see as she bends down to the stove and lights paper that this has cost her. She still hums but I'm pretty sure this is for me and Candy. It works. Candy understands that warmth is coming. I look up at where the pipe enters the ceiling. Black mould and stains and metal discoloured by decades of tightening and releasing. I wonder when was the last time the inside of this chimney was cleaned.

I have to stop imagining death at the end of every action. That's Syndrome. I have to stay here. Like Tildy. In the moment. I wonder if I can hum? I try. Of course I can! I hum a tuneless sequence of notes. Tildy drops a log. She closes the stove door as she watches me. I hum louder. What song? What song can I hum for Tildy? I hum "Freebird." It just comes to me. Tidly's droopy white skin is drawn up into a smile. Her eyes are blue!

She listens on the couch and twirls Candy's ears in her fingers. The room is warming. Loud delicious snaps form the stove.

"I know that song, Mosey!"

Tidly hums along with me, matching some notes, on her own with others. She thinks it's a different song than "Freebird." Maybe a song she learned in church as a girl. We sit like this humming, laughing at each other, through the evening. I switch the songs from time to time. "Shine On You Crazy Diamond." "Bad, Bad Leroy Brown." "Single Ladies (Put a Ring on It)." Each time Tildy listens intently at the start, then slaps her thigh, declaring she knows it. She accompanies me with the same melody each time. Eventually, we grow sleepy. Losing ourselves in the solemn fire.

"I'm sleeping on the couch tonight, Mosey. Keep an eye on the fire. Them rooms back there are froze."

My eyes droop as she pushes logs in on the embers. Droop and drop.

cicada.

I keep thinking spring is coming. I look for signs of thaw. The white mass outside to shrink. I keep thinking it must be late March. It's not. It's mid-August.

Tildy has worked hard to keep us alive. Stacking more wood against the house. Bringing it in when the supply inside gets thin. She has lost weight and hums less. At night she holds the Bible open but doesn't read. She just watches the fire until she falls asleep. I worry for her, not only because she keeps us alive, but because I don't want her to die. I am her baby. I love her.

Candy disappears one day. I try to calm Tildy by humming "Smoke on the Water." Eventually she finds the dog frozen in her bedroom. She lays the body to thaw in front of the stove.

Tildy takes Candy in her arms and wanders out

into the frigid black August afternoon. I have a renewed fear that she will not return. The fire would go out and I would freeze to death in hours. My Tildy. My Tildy. Don't leave me.

I want that bottle now. My grape-sized stomach empties in a snap. There is some rice liquid at the bottom of a jar on my tray. I push my lips toward it but can't reach. The pains are sharp. Not like hunger. More stabbing. I rock back and forth with no clear plan. Either I draw it to me or I fall.

The door opens.

"Somebody's comin', Mosey! Somebody's comin'!"

Tildy lifts me from the high chair and settles on the couch.

"They seen me for sure. Young people. They'll come."

Tildy closes her eyes and mouths a prayer. I need to eat.

A rap at the door.

"Look at that, Mosey. Company."

She lays me on the couch and stands, revealing a baby bottle. I pull the nipple into my mouth and pump.

Tidly opens the door.

"Why, hello!"

I hear a young girl's voice.

"Hi. We're freezing. Can we come in?"

The door opens farther. I can tell that 'cause the

bottle frosts up. Shoes stomp on the floor. The door is shut.

"Come in! Come in! Oh, you poor loves! You look near dead."

Three young men sit on the floor near the stove. One turns.

"This is great. Thank you. Mind if I put another log on?"

They haven't spotted me yet. I am forced to imagine what this looks like. A full-grown man's head on a larval body sucking formula from a baby bottle. I want to scream at myself. I am grotesque. I forgot about all that.

The young man pulls open the stove door, burning his gloves and drives a log in. The other two are staring at me. Eyes as long as test tubes. They look to the girl standing behind me. I can't see her. I hear her though.

"Oh! I'm sorry. What's . . . who's that?"

She is being calm. I hear the struggle. The boys have moved back and are looking anxiously to Tildy. Hurry up. Tell us what we're looking at.

"Oh. That's Mosey."

The boys slowly return their gaze to me. I am too much for them and they move even farther back.

"Do you kids want some food?"

They congregate around the kitchen table. Tildy leaves me on the couch. It's warm here and I have my bottle. I can't see them.

"You folks been stuck out there for long?"

I hear sighs and low whistles.

"Well, you're here now and what's mine is yours."

Silence follows this. I imagine they don't know what to say.

"Thank you."

"Thank you."

"Thank you."

"Thank you."

"Oh, you're good kids."

They eat. I'm not sure what. Something form the warehouse bags.

"I was afraid when I saw you. There's bad people out in the cold and dark. But I guess you know that."

"Oh, we do, ma'am."

More eating sounds. Someone farts and excuses themselves. More eating. I'm beginning to think these kids are a little too polite. A little too wonderful. I bet they want this place and they don't want to share it.

"I'm afraid the back rooms are dangerous cold. We sleep in here. All huddled like penguins."

I hear dishes moving. Wonder what they'll do with those. Tildy doesn't use dishes.

"You're very kind."

"We have money."

I can picture Tildy's hands up. Refusing.

"Let's go sit in front of the fire and listen to your story."

They arrange themselves on the floor in spots far from me. I look in their eyes for Syndrome. Hard to tell. But if they had full-blown Syndrome, they'd be restless. Manic. They'd talk quickly, abandoning subjects, undermining themselves. If they have Syndrome, it's incipient.

"Well. It's what we have, isn't it? We're not going anywhere so we might as well talk about where we come from."

Tildy is interested in them. She wants to talk about the Bible but she'll wait till the end. She wants to get these kids to Heaven and she knows that time is not on their side. The girl looks to the boys and they nod. She will speak for them.

"Well, we come from Angus."

"I know Angus. That's a army town."

The guys nod.

"We grew up there. That's Greg, my brother, and that's Jeff and Paul, his friends. My name is Holly."

"I'm Tildy. Bless you."

Holly smiles. The guys are a little embarrassed.

"We don't remember pre-orbit. So we kinda grew up with it. But our parents and grown-ups have always been freaked out. Ever since I was a kid. We all grew up that way. It was kind of normal. I was in Grade 11 before it got bad. Nothing special. I worked at DQ. Hung around the mall a lot. I wanted to work in a dentist office. That is. Before. I don't think I've seen a dentist for years. There's probably none. I don't know what these guys like. Bikes and scooters. Boards. It's not much of a story up until things got bad."

One of the boys speaks with his eyes cast down, fiddling with his sock.

"Tell her about the Seller."

Tildy hisses.

"Seller? Wicked. Wicked. Wicked. Wicked. Wicked."

They all nod. Holly glances at me.

"Yeah, so, I mean, a Seller came into our school and we had never seen one so we all went to hear him. I thought it was kinda hokey. He was like a rodeo clown or something. I thought it was just, like, a joke. Our parents didn't though. They'd get pissed if we said anything about him. So, anyway, we all went to the airfield to hear him and he went on and on and he had, like, show people with him, like circus people."

That's why they're afraid of me. They think they know exactly what I am.

"I didn't pay much attention and figured it was funny. That night we all come back to the field in our pyjamas and sit around these big fires. The churches were singing songs and I thought it was, like, we all needed to have a break, so that's what we were doing. I thought, Good. That's great. Let's do it. Let's lighten up."

I don't want to look at them I can feel eyes coming to me and leaving quickly, then returning.

"So really, what happens is the clowny guy comes out and says a bunch of stuff then . . ."

Holly goes quiet. I glance up. They are all looking down except Paul, who is glowering at me.

Tildy lays the silence aside.

"I know, child. I know what happens."

I close my eyes. I can't speak. I have no tongue.

"But tell me, Holly, how did you get out?"

Holly takes a deep breath, holds it and exhales.

"Well, I guess, well . . ."

Tildy leaves for a minute, comes back with a tray of biscuits.

"You got away. That's the important thing. You got here. I'm sorry for it all."

She sets the tray on the floor. Greg looks at me, then Tildy.

"We saw some awful things happen. Things—"

"Shush now. It's ok. I don't think there's need for those things ever again."

The kids silently lift biscuits to their lips.

"Amen."

Tildy takes the tray when they're done. She gets Holly to help with blankets and pillows. Soon they are curled up in front of the fire.

Tildy reads from Ecclesiastes until she's sure they're sleeping then she goes down on her knees before me so her face is inches from mine. Her cool hands cradle my head.

"It's been a lovely night, Mosey. Our best night. These kids are good kids."

Tildy kisses my nose and lays her powder-soft cheek on my forehead. I fall asleep to her hum.

In the morning the kids are gathered by the door. They are talking in whispers. I crane around looking for Tildy. She must be in the kitchen. I notice Holly is crying. I listen hard.

"She must have got up in the night."

"Do you think she knew?"

"That she'd freeze in her own bed? Yes, I'm pretty sure."

"That's what she wanted, Holly. C'mon. That's what she wanted to do."

accidents are predatory.

They spend the morning cleaning the house while I weep for Tildy. She waited until I was with someone. She waited until she could find good people to raise me. Oh, Tildy.

Paul walks past me, then takes a step back. He stands over me. I am not Moses. He knows that very well.

"What do we do with this?"

Greg comes to his side and looks down.

"I know what I'd like to do."

Holly moves in between them and me.

"It was Tildy's. She left it for us."

"What if we don't want it?"

"Okay. For now, it's mine. I'll look after it until we figure out what to do."

The boys all look down at me.

"Okay?"

Their eyes are full of the night everyone they ever knew died.

"Just don't leave it alone with us."

"Until you're ready."

Holly pushes the boys back. She looks at me and screws up her face.

"Fuck."

She lifts the empty bottle.

"Seriously. What the fuck are you?"

She sighs through her nose and thinks.

"We live here now."

I nod and try to show a kind face. I honestly don't know what my face looks like any more. Can I even look kind?

Holly rises and returns to the kitchen.

Paul walks by and brings the fire back to life with thin logs. He sits and stares into the fire. He looks over his shoulder then directly at me. His voice is low and nasty.

"I'm gonna pretend you're not here for now. And if that changes, if I have to think about you, then I will drop you in this stove. I promise."

I nod. I want that. Pretend I'm not here. He stands and kicks dirty punk wood in my face.

"I think you're an actual fucking maggot."

He spits on my body.

"Paul!"

Paul steps back with his hands up.

"Okay. Okay. Sorry. I get it."

Holly wipes the bits from my face and rubs with spit. I can tell the way she touches me that deep down she agrees with her brothers.

They move in another room. They are in Tildy's room. I hear a bang. Another. They are moving Tildy's furniture. No. They're moving Tildy.

Don't touch her! Leave her! Cold air and ash swoop into the room. No! I want to go with her! I want to die with her! Put me outside with Tildy! I clench my sides and spring. I shoot myself from the cushion and hit the floor. Air pops out of my lung or lungs and I struggle to return it.

I hear a scream. I snap my head around to see Holly's boot coming at me. She kicks my throat and screams again. I try to call out but only manage a bark. The boys move in and wind up to kick. One raises a heavy log. I recoil and move on the muscled points at my shoulders. I am soon under the couch. I use the floor and the couch bottom against my muscles and move quickly to the back. A hand appears then reaches in. I thrust my head forward and bite down hard on the hand. I taste blood. My mouth fills with it. They are screaming. They are cursing and crying. I will cut you. I will bite you. I roll back and find a groove in the wood floor at the wall. I drop into it and tighten my muscles. A poker is thrust in and it pokes my chest hard.

"Did you get it? Did you get it?"

I lay still. A face peers cautiously under the couch. I watch through half-closed eyes.

"I think so."

Holly is crying.

I wiggle along the groove and draw myself to the wall behind the stove. Too hot. Too hot.

"Well, let's make sure. Pull the couch back. I want this thing in the fuckin' fire."

I roll quickly under the stove. My hair crackles and singes. I come out into the middle of the room. Holly and the boys are busy stabbing the couch with the poker. I move by, drawing my back end up under and pushing forward. I reach the kitchen and spot the door under the sink. It's open. I wiggle through and push the bottles of ancient cleaning liquids aside. They'll see me here. I manage to cram myself into a space between the wall and a box. I stop and listen.

"It's gone!"

"Gone!"

The shrieking begins again.

"Look for it! Find it!"

Things are crashing around in the room. Furniture overturned. Cushions tossed into corners.

"It's not in here!"

"Fuck! Fuck!"

"What do we do?"

"Keep looking!"

"Check the bedroom! Check the kitchen!"

"Hurry! I'm not stayin' in here with that thing!"

They ransack rooms. I push myself hard into the corner, trying to compact my bundled body. I put my face into a spider web. A nest. A thin light cuts in through a crack and I see hundreds of red dots fan across the shroud of silk. I blow into it and the web's upper canopy drifts across my face. The baby spiders trek on my skin. It feels as if my skin is hallucinating. I blow and snort frantically. They have heard me. I am found. Something stabs into my side and I squawk. I spring from the cupboard. I am going to be wild. I am going to scare them to death. I shoot, shrieking into a boy's ankle and bite so completely that my teeth stop deep in bone. Then I twist like a corkscrew. He yells but I am louder. A foot kicks my side and I use the bounce against the wall to fly up. I catch a hand in my teeth and fall with fingers in my throat. A shadow rises but I am too fast. I throw myself upright and spring. I smash a throat and shake my face like a buzz saw. A hand grabs my middle and I attack the wrist. I'm on the ground. I am a poisonous pig. I am a devil stomach.

They have run. Crying comes from the other room. The floor is a violent painting. My lung is sore. The kids are piling furniture in the doorway. Blocking my way. I hear sobbing. Gurgling. One of them is dying. I regurgitate fingers onto the tile. I

can't go back under the cupboard. No point now. The cold is starting to hurt my underside. I need to go up. I flip over so I can see. The door behind me. The stove and fridge. No way up. I don't know if I could climb anything anyway. The frozen tile bites my back. I tear my bindings from ice blood as I turn. The screaming has subsided. Melodramatic teen death. Soon they'll be making a better plan. They'll kill me fast. Nowhere to go but down. I pull against the tack of ice and reach the cupboard again. I go the other direction this time. There's a pile of fetid rags. I mount it to see if it's warmer on top. Snap! A mousetrap bites my side and flies off, hitting a pipe with a high ping. It stings but there's a burning sensation building around me that feels worse. I smell bleach. I've been crawling through bleach. The burn turns into a point against my side. He must have put a hole in me when he stabbed. The bleach is dissolving fat under my skin. I roll quickly on the rags hoping to pull some bleach away. The pain is intensifying. I am moving involuntarily. I turn under the rags, trying to escape. The rags tighten as I twist, constricting my breathing but I can't stop. My body is trying to flee itself.

Goodbye.

Hello. I'm having a dream. I can see a wide band of red. On it, active lines twitching and bouncing. When two lines touch they are joined. Then they become three and so on. Soon all of the lines are part of discrete tangles evenly spaced along the band. I am aware that the band is trying to impress something on me. That the agitation has resulted in this perfect spacing. I see it all as only inevitable because of the way the band has presented itself. If it wanted to make me feel something, it needed to begin somewhere else. Maybe closer to one cluster as it forms. Or stay in the space between. I don't know. I feel disappointed with the band. It has tried too hard to say something. It believed it was magic. I don't know the solution and the band dims. The lines fall to the bottom. This reveals that the dream knew what it was going to say before it said it. And that it used what was nearby to do so. And it ended saying nothing, turning its back and then never having been dreamt.

There is another dream behind it. Much more aggressive, much more certain. It knows that it can fool me into thinking I'm awake in the middle of its story. We'll see. It takes place in a parallel time. There are no orbits or peels or Syndrome. The sky is blue and the clouds are white and we grew up under them and now we live. I still have no arms or legs or sex organs. But I am slightly different than I was. I can move well. I have company. Many others. Thousands, just like me. We are burrowing and feasting on a dead person's leg. We are a maggot horde. It is wonderful to feel part of this mass. My face is a black cowl with snips. My body moves in pulses, forward and back, and this is mirrored thousands of times around me. The leg enters my mouth as strands and excites my body so much that my tail twirls, propelling me. I occasionally cross half-eaten maggots. There is some cannibalism here, but I believe it's caused by ecstatic eating. I accidentally bite into someone. It tastes too sweet. I buckle under to suck more leg. It is becoming liquid under us. It is becoming hot. There is no way we can't win. I pump my face in and feel pus fill my body. This triggers a reaction I don't expect. I tumble off the seething limb and land on the ground. It is colder down here and I soon stop moving. I feel my skin pulling up and my guts falling in. I try to move but I am stiff. All of my excitement is drawn in close to my head. I feel like the mass of maggots is now inside me, an infinite number of infinitely small faces. It is a sensation of profound happiness. I am being built.

The building sensation slows to quick random clicks. It stops. I feel air around me, under my skin. I am a distance from my own skin now. I contract a muscle around my eyes and it starts a choir on my back. The singing is deafening and joyful. The singing drives my old skin into the dirt and carries me into a sky made of a million dazzling suns. It is a dream but I am happy for it. Grateful. It was very finely crafted. When I awake I will be more than I was when I fell asleep.

The rags are keeping me from freezing. They have lessened the corrosion. Some of my lower body has sloughed off into my wrap and smells of putrefaction. I hope the bleach can stem advancing infection. I may well be lying in my last place on earth. I have fought very hard not to die. Did I fight too hard? No. It was my point not to die. It was never my point to live. I am a perfect result of the path I took. I hear movement in the kitchen. The barricade is being disturbed. I lay still and listen.

"I don't see it."

"Oh, it's in there."

"There's knives in a block by the sink. Just run in and pull a couple out. When you see it just carve the fucking maggot."

I hear things being moved. Carefully. Something heavy topples and bounces twice. A crack. The floor cracks under weight. A foot in the kitchen. Another crack. Someone is walking.

They think I'm an animal or a demon. They don't know I can hear them and understand them. I am not going to just offer my soft body to their knives. No. I am buried in caustic rags in a dark confined space. No one is going to take a chance on this. I hear the knife sing a high note as it leaves the block. His feet are so close. I could dive to them from here.

Cram his heel in my mouth and dislodge it with a single flex of jaw. He would fall backwards. No heel. The knife would fall. I'd fly across him like a crow and yank his face clear off with a cinching tear. The rest would of them would faint of fright. They would give up. Wander off. Freeze to death on the hard ash.

I stay. Who can say what would happen? Cupboards are opened. He yells and jumps back every time. The door to the rags is opened. A knife is plunged into my cheek. He pulls the knife but it's imbedded in bone and I come out with it, hanging in the air, twisting and howling. He drops me and bounds back up the barricade.

"I got it! I got it!"

I turn against the blade and ease it from my face. I see two heads peering over the pile. I killed the other two.

"It's still alive! Go back in! Finish it off!"

"No! No!"

A heavy black log sails in over the barricade and shatters beside me.

"What are you doing?"

I fire a dead mouse from my ass. When did it crawl up there?

"Burn the fucking thing!"

The coals are spread across the floor and are melting tile. Another log. There are flames on the wall and in the box I hid behind.

THE *n*-BODY PROBLEM

I have to go down. These two will die. They will end up combined and moving like Paula and Petra in the ashes of this house. I will escape down.

I return to the rags and press my cheek. I will do this until the flames are close. I have to slow the bleeding. I see a dark triangle in the back corner of the adjacent cupboard. I launch myself at it and slip through. There is a wide plastic pipe. I try to move along it like an inchworm but the surface is too smooth and I slip off. Hit the concrete floor very hard and have to lie still. They are burning the house down to kill me. I manage to fill my lung again and roll over. I hear the floor above me crackling and the air in the kitchen start to hammer. This house will go up fast and all the children will die. Fire goes up. I go down. The house will come down eventually. I try to move. My skin has dissolved into linen. The hole in my side is like a deep canker. I have had a long knife in my face today. My one lung is scorched with ammonia. The children will die in my funeral pyre. I look for the place I want to die.

Discs of fire slip in and out under the door at the top of the stairs. Its blue-tip fingers have lifted all the tile. I would like to picture the kids not escaping but they might, after all. I feel the expectation that I should release them. That I should give life back while mine goes. But really, what can I practically do? I let you live. I can't even say it. I have no tongue and even if I could, the roar of the fire would drown my voice. And even if it didn't, even if it was heard, say, in the sky above the house, spoken by birds and repeated by rabbits, there is nothing in the words to shrink the flame or dim the heat. Even if there were birds and rabbits to speak them. So I am safe to say that they should live, that that is my last wish because I know that they will not. The fire is bounding down the stairs like a Slinky. Part of the house leans and opens an edge. They will burn in here or freeze out there. I hope that they are safe.

I feel solved now. There are two sumps in the floor. One has a pump the other not. The sump was designed hundreds of years ago and dedicated as a tomb. I roll. I approach the sump at an angle so my bottom enters first. Skin is gone in places and seared tough in others. I decide not to feel pain for a sec. My bottom hits crumpled chicken wire that compresses under my weight. I slide in. I am a nematode in a grub's back. What I am doing is repeated in nature. I fill the sump. The floor is level with my chin. It is warmer in here, close as I can be to the hot centre of the earth. I feel colossal. I think that in the moments before you die, your body assumes things. I fit perfectly in this hole.

all good things.

Stone in water. Corner in water. Joists in water. Kids in water. Sub-basement in water. Water in water. Stone in ash. Corner in ash. Joists in ash. Kids in ash. Sub-basement in ash. Ash in ash.

Plastics bent. Stone in plastic. Corner in plastic water. Kids in ash. Sub-basement in plastic. Plastic in plastic. Joists. Water. Water. Stone. Plastic. Kids. Ash. Window is Q. Stairs are ash. Window.

I can't say this story right now.

Brick is over. Water is over. Window is Q. Ash is ash. Kids are ash. Sub-basement is ash. Water is ash. Plastic is black. Ash is black. Sub-basement is black. Window is black. Black in water. Water in black water. Brick is over. Brick is over. Water is plastic. Water is black plastic. Puddle in plastic. Water in ash. Ash is over. Puddle in brick. Kids in puddle.

Sub-basement in puddle. Window is Q. Ash is Q. Q is over.

Some minutes in.

The man is a maggot with no arms or legs or genitals wrapped in a sopping foul rag. He has risen on flood waters from a sump in a burned-out basement. A single lung is emptied of water and filled with air for ballast. The man is a bandaged toe. He is conveyed on slow-moving ash. It is enough to call trees by name. Birch. Ash. Maple. Poplar. Cedar. White Pine. Blue Spruce.

More minutes in.

Jackson Pine. An entire cloud. Sand in ash. If the water recedes it will leave a wide gasket of brackish gel. The bandaged toe is turned by a rock. There is a thing called a bunny. Not here. Not now. But there is. The water isn't revealing its vertical face. Its pirate hat. But there it is. Half in and half out. An entire cloud.

Not minutes. Not right now.

The culverts clear the water from the land and the graded roads breach like whales. The trucks are all in pots of ash and the silos are upright. The deer are a carcass and the coyote are alone. There are things that people made by hand and what they are. Pollen is picked from bark and sound is watching this spread. There is no rhythm to things. Not right now.

I am lying on a flat stone. The ash flow moves

around it. I have lost all sensation. My nerve endings have been cut by bleach. I have to share my lung with my septic heart. My brain. Oh, well.

The sky is mighty blue. So blue it looks like sky. The sun is fire. Burning gas. I feel this on my flat rock. The ultra violet light. The radiation reaching my sides by bouncing off the flat rock. I have to turn my face from the direct rays. I am a bean from a can. I am sniffing the sun as it lands. This is a real sky. I turn on the rock to pull my robes off. I am a bean from a can. Is this the real sky? I turn to the east. A dark cloud. I smell rainwater.

It is the thing we haven't seen in ten long years. It is the thing we were told might never return. Our bodies in the sky prevented it. The red takes up the orange and they curve. A yellow path lined with green. Blue. Indigo. Violet. We have left the sky. Returned its flags. Apologized.

Rainbow.

ABOUT THE AUTHOR

Tony Burgess writes fiction and for film. He lives in Stayner with his wife, Rachel, and their two children, Griffin and Camille.

EMB
RACE
THE
ODD

THE MONA LISA SACRIFICE
BOOK ONE OF THE BOOK OF CROSS
PETER ROMAN

For thousands of years, Cross has wandered the earth, a mortal soul trapped in the undying body left behind by Christ. But now he must play the part of reluctant hero, as an angel comes to him for help finding the Mona Lisa—the real Mona Lisa that inspired the painting. Cross's quest takes him into a secret world within our own, populated by characters just as strange and wondrous as he is. He's haunted by memories of Penelope, the only woman he truly loved, and he wants to avenge her death at the hands of his ancient enemy, Judas. The angel promises to deliver Judas to Cross, but nothing is ever what it seems, and when a group of renegade angels looking for a new holy war show up, things truly go to hell.

AVAILABLE NOW
978-1-77148-145-8

CHIZINEPUB.COM

ZOMBIE VERSUS FAIRY FEATURING ALBINOS

JAMES MARSHALL

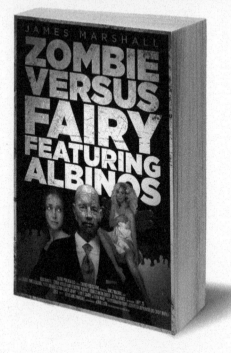

In a PERFECT world where everyone DESTROYS everything and eats HUMAN FLESH, one ZOMBIE has had enough: BUCK BURGER. When he rebels at the natural DISORDER, his marriage starts DETERIORATING and a doctor prescribes him an ANTI-DEPRESSANT. Buck meets a beautiful GREEN-HAIRED pharmacist fairy named FAIRY_26 and quickly becomes a pawn in a COLD WAR between zombies and SUPERNATURAL CREATURES. Does sixteen-year-old SPIRITUAL LEADER and pirate GUY BOY MAN make an appearance? Of course! Are there MIND-CONTROLLING ALBINOS? Obviously! Is there hot ZOMBIE-ON-FAIRY action? Maybe! WHY AREN'T YOU READING THIS YET?

AVAILABLE NOW
978-1-77148-141-0

IMAGINARIUM 2013
THE BEST CANADIAN SPECULATIVE WRITING
EDITED BY SANDRA KASTURI & SAMANTHA BEIKO

INTRODUCTION BY TANYA HUFF
COVER ART BY GMB CHOMICHUK

A yearly anthology from ChiZine Publications, gathering the best Canadian fiction and poetry in the speculative genres (SF, fantasy, horror, magic realism) published in the previous year. *Imaginarium 2012* (edited by Sandra Kasturi and Halli Villegas, with a provocative introduction by Steven Erikson) was nominated for a Prix Aurora Award.

AVAILABLE NOW
978-1-77148-145-8

CHIZINEPUB.COM

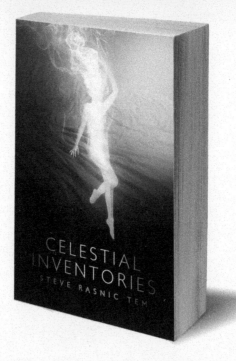

TELL MY SORROWS TO THE STONES
CHRISTOPHER GOLDEN

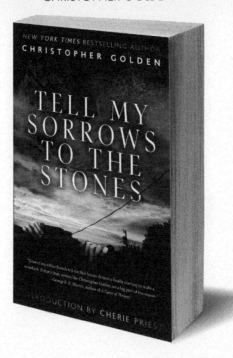

A circus clown willing to give anything to be funny. A spectral gunslinger who must teach a young boy to defend the ones he loves. A lonely widower making a farewell tour of the places that meant the world to his late wife. A faded Hollywood actress out to deprive her ex-husband of his prize possession. A grieving mother who will wait by the railroad tracks for a ghostly train that always has room for one more. A young West Virginia miner whose only hope of survival is a bedtime story. These are just some of the characters to be found in *Tell My Sorrows to the Stones*.

AVAILABLE NOW
978-1-77148-153-3

CHIZINEPUB.COM

THE SUMMER IS ENDED AND WE ARE NOT YET SAVED
JOEY COMEAU

Martin is going to Bible Camp for the summer. He's going to learn archery and swimming, and he's going to make new friends. He's pretty excited, but that's probably because nobody told him that this is a horror novel.

THE DELPHI ROOM
MELIA MCCLURE

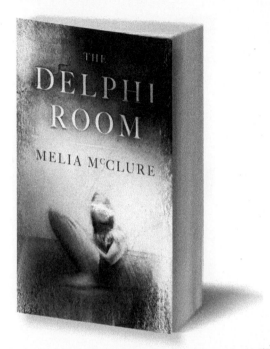

Is it possible to find love after you've died and gone to Hell? For oddball misfits Velvet and Brinkley, the answer just might be yes. After Velvet hangs herself and winds up trapped in a bedroom she believes is Hell, she comes in contact with Brinkley, the man trapped next door. Through mirrors that hang in each of their rooms, these disturbed cinemaphiles watch the past of the other unfold—the dark past that has led to their present circumstances. As their bond grows and they struggle to figure out the tragic puzzles of their lives and deaths, Velvet and Brinkley are in for more surprises. By turns quirky, harrowing, funny and surreal, *The Delphi Room* explores the nature of reality and the possibilities of love.

WIKIWORLD
PAUL DI FILIPPO

Wikiworld contains a wild assortment of Di Filippo's best and most recent work. The title story, a radical envisioning of near-future sociopolitical modes, received accolades from both Cory Doctorow and Warren Ellis. In addition, there are alternate history adventures such as "Yes We Have No Bananas" (which critic Gary Wolfe called "a new kind of science fiction"); homages to icons such as Stanislaw Lem ("The New Cyberiad"); collaborations with Rudy Rucker and Damien Broderick; and a posthuman odyssey ("Waves and Smart Magma").

THINGS WITHERED
SUSIE MOLONEY

The first story collection from this award-winning author. A middle-aged realtor tries to get ahead any way she can. A bad girl pays for cheating with a married man. A wife with a dark past lives in fear of being exposed. The bad acts of a little old lady come home to roost. A young man with no direction finds power behind the wheel of a haunted truck. From behind the pretty drapes of the average suburban home, madness peers out. Nine stories of suburban darkness prove that life can turn on you, or you can turn on it.

AVAILABLE OCTOBER 2013
978-1-77148-161-8

CHIZINEPUB.COM

WILD FELL
MICHAEL ROWE

The crumbling summerhouse called Wild Fell, soaring above the desolate shores of Blackmore Island, has weathered the violence of the seasons for more than a century. Built for his family by a 19th-century politician of impeccable rectitude, the house has kept its terrible secrets and its darkness sealed within its walls. For a hundred years, the townspeople of Alvina have prayed that the darkness inside Wild Fell would stay there, locked away from the light.

AVAILABLE NOVEMBER 2O13
978-1-77148-159-5

GAMIFICATION/C-MONKEYS
KEITH HOLLIHAN

This is a double novella "flip book" pairing a modern corporate suspense story about the cover-up of a CEO's illicit affair, with a 1970s-era science fiction thriller about an oil company's environmental disaster. It is an exploration of the paranoia inherent in business and the thin line between competition and conspiracy.

AVAILABLE NOVEMBER 2013
978-1-77148-151-9

MORE FROM CHIZINE

ALSO AVAILABLE FROM CHIZINE PUBLICATIONS